CONTENTS

PAGE

ILLUSTRATIONS

INTRODUCTION

The original story, *Moby Dick,* or *The White Whale,* written by Herman Melville, represents a work of research seldom equalled by writers of stories. However, the original volume contains some 219,000 words, divided into 134 chapters, and a considerable Appendix.

As originally written, the book has many drawbacks for the young, or less expert, reader. It is long, rambling, and contains many expressions that are impossible except for the reader of large experience. However, it is one of the literary classics and, as such, should be made available to as many readers as possible. Every young person should have the satisfaction of having read it.

It was with that in mind that I undertook to rewrite the story. It has been retold in about 38,000 words, divided into 32 chapters.

The original story was written in the first person, which makes it difficult for the young reader to identify himself with any of the characters. The present interpretation is written in the third person and is, therefore, much easier to follow. It becomes an adventure story with a strong appeal.

Where it was thought necessary to interpret the thought in language different from the original, I have employed my own method of expression freely.

My effort has been to make this a clear, readable story of adventure while adhering strictly to the ideas of the original author. I have tried to present a story that flows along easily and in proper sequence. Much of what I regard as extraneous matter has been eliminated.

It is my hope that young people will learn to love *The Story of Moby Dick* as much as I love it.

FRANK L. BEALS

The Quarter-Deck

"Mr. Starbuck," Captain Ahab called to the first mate, "send everybody aft!"

"Sir!" exclaimed the mate, too surprised at the order to obey at once.

"Send everybody aft!" repeated the captain. Then, without waiting for the mate to give an order, he called, "You, in the mastheads there, come down!"

Captain Ahab had been walking back and forth on the quarter-deck. He had lost one leg and he used one made of ivory. This gave him an odd gait. His brow was wrinkled for his mind was on Moby Dick, the White Whale. After he had been walking back and forth for some time he stopped at the ship's side. There he placed the tip of his ivory leg in an auger hole. With one hand he took hold of a rope.

When the ship's company had gathered, the men looked at the captain nervously. His brow was drawn into a deep frown. He looked over the side of the ship, and at the crew. He again began his pacing back and forth. With bent head he paced, not noticing the whispering men. Suddenly he stopped and faced them.

"What do you do when you see a whale, men?" he called to them.

"Sing out for him," answered several voices.

"Good!" cried Ahab in wild approval. His question had stirred the men and caught their attention.

"And what do you do next, men?"

"Lower a boat and after him!"

"And what tune do you sing as you pull, men?"

"A dead whale or a stove boat!"

The old man's face lighted up at every cry. The men looked questioningly at each other. The captain swung around on his ivory leg.

"Before now you have heard me give orders about a white whale. Do you see this Spanish ounce of gold?" and he held a bright coin in the sun. "It's a sixteen dollar piece, men. Do you see it? Mr. Starbuck, hand me that topmaul."

While the mate was getting the hammer, Ahab, without speaking, slowly rubbed the gold piece against the skirt of his jacket. He took the topmaul from the first mate and walked to the mainmast. He held up the coin. He said:

"The one who sights a white headed whale with a wrinkled brow and a crooked jaw; the one who sights a white headed whale with three holes in his starboard fluke; the one who sights that same white whale shall have this gold ounce, my boys!"

"Hurrah, hurrah!" cried the seamen as the captain nailed the gold piece to the mast.

"It's a white whale, I say," called Ahab as he threw down the topmaul, "a white whale. Skin your eyes for him, men. Look for white water. Sing out if you see but a bubble, sing out!"

Tashtego, Daggoo, and Queequeg, the three harpooners, had watched the whole show with more interest and surprise than the others.

"Captain Ahab," said Tashtego, "that white whale must be the one called Moby Dick."

"Moby Dick?" shouted Ahab excitedly. "Do you know the white whale, Tash?"

"Has he a queer spout, too?" asked Daggoo.

"And has he many irons in his side?" Queequeg wanted to know.

"Yes, Queequeg, many harpoons are twisted in his side. His spout is a big one, like a whole shock of wheat, Daggoo. Death and devils, men, it is Moby Dick you have seen! Moby Dick! Moby Dick!"

"Captain Ahab," said Starbuck who had been standing with Stubb and Flask, "I have heard of Moby Dick. But was it Moby Dick that took off your leg?"

"Aye, it was Moby Dick! Aye, it was that accursed white whale! And I'll chase him around the world before I'll give him up. That is what you are on my ship for, men, to chase that white whale until he spouts black blood. You look like brave men. Are you with me?"

"Aye, aye!" shouted harpooners and seamen as they moved closer to the excited captain.

"God bless you, men, God bless you!" almost sobbed the captain. "But what's the matter with you, Mr. Starbuck? Why the long face? Are you not game for Moby Dick?"

"I am game for Moby Dick and his crooked jaw, and I am game for the jaws of death, too, Captain Ahab, if they come as a part of the business we follow. But I came here to hunt whales, not to help you get revenge. How much do you think your revenge will bring you in the Nantucket market? Will it add to our profits?"

"My revenge will bring a great premium here!" and Captain Ahab thumped his chest with closed fist.

"Revenge on a dumb brute that simply struck from blind instinct," cried Starbuck. "You are mad!"

"The white whale dares me. He took off my leg. I hate him and I will have revenge upon him. I'd strike the sun if it insulted me." Ahab shook his fist at the sun.

"I'll kill the white whale!" he shouted.

"God keep me!—keep us all!" murmured Starbuck slowly.

Captain Ahab went into his cabin.

Ship and Crew

The *Pequod,* named for a tribe of Massachusetts Indians, was as queer a ship as ever sailed the seas. She was small. She had been seasoned and weather stained in the storms of the four oceans. Her bows looked as though she wore a long beard because pieces of polished ivory hung from them. The guard rails were trimmed with the sharp teeth of many sperm whales. The teeth had been placed in the guard rails to hold the ropes of sails and spars.

The decks of the *Pequod* were worn and wrinkled like the face of a very old woman. Her masts, which had been cut somewhere on the coasts of Japan, stood stiffly upright. Her last captain had outfitted her in many odd ways not seen on other ships. All over her were prizes taken from enemies.

Instead of a steering wheel she had a tiller, all in one piece, carved from the long narrow lower jaw of a whale.

Altogether, there was something a little sad about the *Pequod.*

7

Captain **Ahab** was like a man cast from solid bronze. A white, slender scar ran from his white hair down across his tanned face and neck and passed from sight under his collar. It was like the streak which a stroke of lightning leaves on a tree.

On each side of the quarter-deck there was an auger hole bored about half an inch into a plank. The captain could stick the end of his ivory leg into one of these holes and steady himself.

When he looked over the ship it was with a master-eye. When he was under great strain he smoked his pipe to calm his nerves.

Besides Captain Ahab, the ship had three officers, or mates. They were Starbuck, first mate; Stubb, second mate; and Flask, third. In addition to his regular duties on the ship each mate had command of a whaleboat.

Starbuck, the first mate, a native of Nantucket, was a very religious man. He was fearless when hunting whales, but he did not believe in taking foolish chances. He felt that his job was to kill whales, not to be killed by them.

Stubb, the second mate, was a Cape Cod man. He was tall, slender, happy-go-lucky, and he met the dangers of the sea without fear. He was good-humored, easy-going, careless. When fighting a whale he handled his lance easily and coolly. With a short black pipe in his mouth, he was a picture of calmness and courage.

Flask, the third mate, was from Martha's Vineyard. He was a short, stout, ruddy young fellow. He was always mad at whales and wanted to destroy them. He followed whaling just for the fun of it. On the *Pequod* he was called King-Post.

In addition to the regular members of the crew each whaleboat carried a harpooner. The harpooner ranked next to an officer. He took his meals in the captain's cabin, and he slept in the after part of the ship. The harpooner was an important person on a whaling ship.

The *Pequod* carried three harpooners.

Queequeg, Mr. Starbuck's harpooner, was the queerest of all the queer members of the crew of the *Pequod*. He was the son of the king of the island of Kokovoko. Such a face as he had! It was covered with squares tattooed in all colors of the rainbow. Any of the skin that was not tattooed was of a purplish yellow hue.

For hair on his head he had only a wisp, twisted into a scalp knot. This fell over his forehead. The rest of his body was as fearsome as his face. His chest, arms, and back were covered with the same tattooed squares as his face. Even his legs looked as though green frogs were running up them.

He stood six feet two inches in his bare feet.

He carried a little shiny ebony figure which was his idol. He prayed to it by kneeling and burning a small fire in front of it. When through praying to the idol he would pick it up in one hand and drop it into his pocket.

He smoked a pipe that was part pipe and part hatchet, or tomahawk.

Tashtego, Stubb's harpooner, was a fullblooded Indian from Martha's Vineyard. His long black hair, high cheek bones, and black, flashing eyes showed his race. When he threw his harpoon, it was as sure and went as straight to its mark as an arrow from the bow of one of his ancestors.

Daggoo, Flask's harpooner, came from Africa. He was a giant, six feet five inches tall, with the soft step of a lion. In his ears he wore golden hoops for ear-rings. Beside him Flask looked like a small chess man.

The rest of the crew came from the islands of the seven seas, and from all of the ends of the earth. They were: black little Pip from Alabama; Dough-Boy, the cook; five Nantucket sailors; and sailors of all nationalities, Dutch, French, Icelandish, Maltese, Sicilian, Chinese, Tahitan, Portuguese, Danish, English, Irish, and Indian.

The Pipe

"Going down to my cabin is like going into a tomb," Captain Ahab muttered to himself. "This narrow passage is like the path to my grave. My berth is like the grave itself."

As the spring weather grew warmer, and the *Pequod* left the icebergs behind, Captain Ahab spent more and more time on the quarter-deck.

Sometimes he just stood and looked at the far horizon, the tip of his ivory leg in its auger hole, his faithful pipe in his mouth. At other times he sat on an ivory stool and watched the sails and the men aloft. At still other times he paced restlessly back and forth across the quarter-deck, his eyes on the water, looking for signs of a whale.

The days, warm and clear, were followed by nights on which the blue heavens were filled with stars that shone like diamonds. This fine weather had its effect on Captain Ahab. He stayed much on deck. He visited his cabin only when it was necessary. He smoked all the time.

When the quiet of night hung over the waters Ahab

came out of his cabin. In moving along the narrow passage to the deck he gripped the iron rail to help him make his crippled way to the quarter-deck. Once there he stumped back and forth. On a certain night Stubb came up to hint that the captain was disturbing the sleep of the crew. He suggested that the ivory leg be muffled in some way.

"And so you would wad me as you would a cannon ball, would you?" demanded Ahab. "Go away! Get below to your nightly grave! Down, dog, to your kennel!"

For a moment Stubb stood speechless. He was too surprised and stunned by the old man's outburst to answer at once.

"I am not used to being spoken to in that way, Sir," he finally blurted out. "I don't like it."

"Get out!" gritted Ahab between clenched teeth as he moved away quickly.

"No, Sir, not yet," said Stubb boldly. "I will not be called a dog!"

"Then be called ten times a mule, a donkey! Begone or I'll clear the world of you!"

"I never was so spoken to before without giving a hard blow in return for it," muttered Stubb as he went down the cabin passage. "Shall I go back and strike him, or shall I kneel down and pray for him?"

"He's the queerest old man I ever sailed with," Stubb

went on, speaking to himself. "There's something on his mind. He's in bed only about three hours out of twenty-four, and he doesn't sleep even then. His conscience must be troubling him worse than a toothache. I don't know what has him in its grip, but whatever it is, I hope I don't catch it. Dough-Boy says the old man goes into the after-hold every night. I wonder what for. Anyhow, its time for me to snooze. I have two commandments of my own. One is, 'don't think,' and the other is, 'sleep when you can,' But he called me a dog and a donkey! He might as well have kicked me! But now for my hammock. I'll think it over tomorrow."

Ahab stood leaning over the rail after Stubb had gone. After a time he called a sailor and sent him below for an ivory stool and a pipe. When these were brought to him Ahab sat on the stool and lighted the pipe. As he sat and smoked thick clouds came from his mouth in quick, steady puffs. The wind blew the smoke back into his face.

"Smoking no longer soothes me," Ahab said to himself as he stood up. "Oh, pipe, I am afraid your charm is gone, and it will go hard with you. Here I have been smoking and puffing into the wind. What business have I with a pipe, anyhow? I'll smoke no more!"

He tossed the still lighted pipe into the sea. As it struck the water the fire hissed once, then it was gone. Ahab, his hat pulled over his eyes, paced the planks.

The Cabin Table

"Dinner, Mr. Starbuck," Captain Ahab said in an even voice.

It was noon and the captain had been taking an observation of the sun. He figured out the latitude on a tablet fastened to the upper part of his ivory leg. He was so busy with his figuring that he did not move when Dough-Boy thrust his pale loaf-of-bread face above the deck and shouted, "Dinner!"

In a short time, however, he took hold of a rope and swung himself to the deck.

Mr. Starbuck waited a few minutes. He then took a few turns across the deck. He stopped at the cabin passage and called out pleasantly:

"Dinner, Mr. Stubb."

After Mr. Starbuck had gone below Stubb walked about for a while. He pretended to be busy. Finally he followed Mr. Starbuck down the cabin passage-way, calling out as he went:

"Dinner, Mr. Flask."

Flask, who was now alone on the quarter-deck, kicked off his shoes and danced the sailor's hornpipe. He tossed up his cap, and danced down the passage toward the cabin. However, before entering he stopped and became sober in face and manner. When he stepped into the cabin he was very serious.

Captain Ahab sat at the head of the table. As he carved, each of the officers watched his knife. No one spoke a word. When he had carved the first piece of meat, he held it between knife and fork, and motioned for Starbuck's plate. Each of the officers was served in the same way.

Each officer cut his meat carefully to avoid making a noise. Not one of them let his knife strike against his plate. Each chewed his meat without making a sound. A heavy silence hung over the cabin. No one talked. Talking was not forbidden, it was just that the captain never spoke. For that reason the others were silent too. Any sort of noise was welcome, even a noise made by a rat in the hold. No one of the officers served himself. Each waited to be served by the captain. And yet, no one was forbidden to help himself if he wanted to do so.

Poor Flask! He did not even attempt to help himself to butter. The result was that he never had any butter.

Flask was the last one down to dinner. He was the first on deck after it was over. Starbuck and Stubb always reached the table before Flask. They left it after he had gone. Therefore, they fared better than he. He complained that since he had become an officer he was always hungry.

"I am an officer," he said, "but I wish that I could fish out a chunk of old fashioned beef like I used to do in the forecastle."

For each meal the table in the cabin was set twice. The first table was for the captain and his three mates. When they were through the canvas cloth was removed from the table. Then the three harpooners sat down to eat.

They were not silent. They made as much noise with their knives as they liked. They even made lots of noise chewing their food. They had huge appetites. They ate all the food set before them and called on Dough-Boy for more. He had to bring great amounts of corned beef to satisfy their hunger. If he did not bring it fast enough Tashtego speeded him up by jabbing a fork at his back.

At the table Queequeg and Tashtego sat opposite each other. But Daggoo was too tall, too big to sit at the table. He sat on the floor. However, in eating he was not greedy like the others. His habits were dainty. If he was a savage, at least he was a noble savage.

Queequeg was a lusty eater with a smack to his lips that kept poor Dough-Boy in a state of terror. When Tashtego called out that he would pick Dough-Boy's bones, the poor fellow trembled and his teeth chattered.

Though these barbarians dined in the cabin they did not stay there after they had finished eating. As soon as their meal was over they went on deck.

Except at mealtime the captain kept the cabin to himself.

Mastheads and Night

"This ship is captained by a madman," said Mr. Starbuck to himself as he stood leaning against the mainmast. It was night and no one stood watch in the mastheads.

"He will come to a bad end, and I must help him to it," continued Starbuck. "He's a horrible old man! He lords it over all of us. I hate him, and yet I pity him. At the same time, all I can do is obey him. Yet there is hope. The White Whale has the whole round, watery world in which to swim. Maybe we shall miss him."

The wind had risen steadily and the rain poured. Suddenly Mr. Starbuck shouted into the night:

"Hands by the halyards! In topgallant sails! Stand by to reef topsails! A squall! A squall! Jump, my jollies!"

Little Pip hid under the windlass. He cried out:

"Jollies? What jollies! Crash! There goes the jibstay. Duck lower, Pip, here comes the royal yard. Hold on hard! What a squall! And the old man swore 'em in to hunt the White Whale! Oh, Lord, have mercy on this small boy!"

The squall blew itself out. Quiet and peace once more settled over the ship. She sailed on into the bright sunshine of the following day.

The sailors who were to be on watch climbed to the mastheads to keep a lookout for Moby Dick, the White Whale.

The masthead of the old-time sailing ship was very different from the crow's nest of a modern ship. On a whale boat, the sailor who stood watch at the masthead had to stand on two parallel sticks known as the topgallant crosstrees. He was tossed about by the sea much as he would have been tossed if he had been standing on a bull's horns. There was nothing to protect the sailor from wind, rain, or sleet. He could not even sit down. He had to stand and take what came.

The *Pequod* had three masts. Near the top of each was the masthead. During daylight there were always three sailors on the lookout for whales. At night no one stood watch at the mastheads.

Moby Dick

The members of the crew of the *Pequod* had taken an oath against that murderous monster, Moby Dick, the White Whale. They had made the feud of Ahab, the captain, their feud. They hunted the whale as they would have hunted a personal enemy.

At times Moby Dick had been seen in those seas where sperm whale fishermen hunted. However, only a few of the fishermen had ever seen him.

The sperm whale was known as the worst of all the monsters in the sea. The sperm whale was the terror of all ocean creatures. Even the sharks were afraid of the sperm whale. So terrible was his name that it was not easy to find sailors who would risk their lives hunting him. However, there were men who were glad to give chase to Moby Dick. These were the men who welcomed battle with the monster.

The sperm whales moved fast. In a short period of time they could move from one part of the ocean to another far away. Sailors believed that sperm whales had found the North-west Passage long before any man found it.

Sailors believed that Moby Dick could not be killed. They had some reason for this belief. He had lived through many battles. In these battles spears had been planted in his sides, but he always swam away the victor.

Moby Dick was different from all other sperm whales. He was huge. He was larger than others of his kind. His white wrinkled forehead and high white hump made him stand out from the others. Those who knew him could recognize him by these signs, even from far away. But it was his ugly lower jaw that struck terror to the hearts of those who came near him.

Moby Dick was smart. It was said that he was smarter than any other creature of the deep. He would make believe that he was swimming away from a whaleboat as though afraid, only to turn suddenly, bear down on the boat and smash it to splinters.

Many men had lost their lives trying to kill the White Whale. In the case of every man killed by him there were signs of great skill.

Captain Ahab's fight with Moby Dick had been a fierce battle. The captain's three boats had been smashed. Men and oars had been whirled about him in the sea. Ahab grabbed a knife and swam at the whale. He tried to take the life of that great monster with a six inch blade.

Suddenly Moby Dick swept his sickle shaped jaw under Ahab. He reaped away a leg as easily as a mower would cut a blade of grass in a field. Moby Dick cut off Ahab's leg as though he had been planning to do it for a long time.

Ever after Ahab hated Moby Dick. He lived only to get even for the loss of his leg. When he thought of the whale's white hump he longed for the time when he could get even.

After the loss of his leg Ahab lay for long months in his hammock. He suffered great pain. But he hated the White Whale so much that he would not die. So great was his hatred of the whale that for months he was a madman.

When, finally, he was able to be on deck again, he once more gave his orders calmly. His men were glad that the madness had left him. But he only looked as though the madness had left him. Inside him the madness of hate, and a desire to get even, went on.

Ahab knew that he was mad. But he was cunning and clever enough to hide his madness from most of the men. He did it so that he could find a way to get even with his living enemy, Moby Dick. This idea was fixed in his mind. He thought of little else. Thus Moby Dick became the only reason for hunting on the part of the *Pequod* and her crew.

Secret of the Night

"Hist! Cabaco! Did you hear that noise?" whispered a sailor to the man nearest him.

"Take the bucket, will you! What noise?" was the whispered reply.

It was night. The men were standing in line from a fresh water butt in the center of the ship to the scuttle butt near the tap-rail. They handed buckets from one to another to fill the scuttle butt. The moon shone brightly.

Some of the men stood on the quarter-deck. They were careful not to speak or rustle their feet on the deck. They were afraid of disturbing the captain in his cabin below. The men were silent. The buckets passed from hand to hand.

"There it is again, under the hatches! Don't you hear it?" whispered the first sailor.

"What noise? Take the bucket, will you!" repeated Cabaco.

"It sounds like a cough."

"Cough, your eye! Pass along that return bucket."

"There it is! It sounds like two or three sleepers turning over."

"Stop it, will you, Shipmate!" growled Cabaco. "It's the three biscuits you ate for supper turning over inside you. That's all it is. Look out for the bucket!"

"Say what you will, Shipmate, I heard it. I have sharp ears."

"So you have. You're the lad who heard the click of the old woman's knitting needles fifty miles at sea from Nantucket. You're the lad with the sharp ears, all right!"

"Laugh if you like, but you will see what turns up. Now listen, Cabaco. There's somebody down in the afterhold, and he has not been on deck. I think old Ahab knows something about it, too. One morning watch I heard Stubb and Flask talking. From what they said I know there is something going on in the afterhold."

"Aw, fish! Look out for the bucket!" and with these words Cabaco ended the whispering.

Ahab's Charts

"I have located the whale on my charts," muttered Ahab long after midnight. "He shall not get away from me."

Ahab had been studying a large roll of yellowish, wrinkled sea charts which were spread out on a table. He had studied the lines and shadings on the charts. With a slow, steady pencil he had traced more courses over spaces that had been blank. Sometimes he studied one of the old logbooks piled beside him. These logbooks had the records of the places and seasons in which sperm whales had been seen or caught. He studied by the light of a heavy pewter lamp hung on chains over his head.

Ahab knew all the tides and currents of the ocean. Knowing these he could tell the driftings of the sperm whale's food. He could tell almost to the day when the whales would be at a certain place.

When they go from one feeding place to another, sperm whales swim in what are called 'veins.' They follow a given line just as exactly as a ship follows her course. By finding these 'veins' on his maps, Ahab could tell just where and when he would be most likely to find whales.

He had a pet way of naming the place where he expected to find Moby Dick. He called it the 'Season-on-the-Line.' Any spot at which the White Whale had stopped year after year he called the 'Season-on-the-Line.' These were the places where most of the deadly fights had been fought.

And so Ahab's mad mind followed the doings of Moby Dick. When he finally slept his hands were clenched tight. So strong was his feeling about Moby Dick, he would even start from his sleep fighting an imaginary whale.

Then back to his charts he would go to find his enemy, Moby Dick, again.

Away She Blows

The silence which hung over the ship was broken by a wild, long drawn out wail.

"There she blows! There! There! There! She blows! She blows!" screamed Tashtego pointing frantically. He hung high up in the crosstrees. His body leaned forward, and one hand pointed like a wand. His cries were wild.

Captain Ahab had been going about doing his work every day. He made believe that he was looking for many kinds of whales. In this way he hid from the crew his one purpose. That purpose was to hunt only Moby Dick. While he had already told the men that he was hunting the White Whale, he dared not let them think this was the only reason for the trip.

The afternoon was cloudy and hot. The seamen moved slowly about the deck. Queequeg and his helper were busy weaving a mat. No one spoke and a silence hung over the ship. Tashtego was high up in the crosstrees. His body leaned forward. Suddenly he began his wild cries.

"There she blows! There! There! There!"

"Where away?" called Ahab who was on the quarter-deck.

"On the lee beam! A school of whales! About two miles off!"

At once all was commotion.

The sperm whale spouts every few minutes. It is by this regular spouting that sailors can tell the sperm whale from all other whales.

"There go flukes!" cried Tashtego as the whales dived into deep water.

"Quick, Steward," called Ahab, "give me the time!"

Dough-Boy hurried to the captain's cabin and came back with the exact minute.

The ship now rolled gently before the wind. The whales were out of sight below the water. Tashtego came down from the crosstrees and another man took his place. Some of the sails were lowered. The three whaleboats were pushed over the side. They hung there on the cranes and the men waited for the order to lower them into the water.

Lower Away

As the boats hung over the water a sudden shout startled the waiting men.

"All ready there, Fedallah?" called Ahab to a man who came on deck wearing a white turban.

"Ready!" was the half hissed reply.

The men looked at Ahab. He now had five husky Chinese around him. Without waiting for an order they ran across the deck. They went to the captain's boat and made it ready to swing over the side.

The man who wore the white turban was tall and dark. One white tooth stuck out through his drawn lips. He wore a jacket and trousers of black cotton cloth. A white turban covered his long black hair which was braided and wound round and round. The Chinese were dressed in the same way, except for the turban.

The sailors looked at these strangers with awe.

"Lower away then!" shouted Ahab as soon as Fedallah, a Parsee from India, had hissed his reply. "Lower away there, I say."

There was thunder in Ahab's voice. In spite of their amazement the sailors sprang over the rail. The three boats dropped into the sea. The sailors leaped down the side of the rolling ship and into the boats being tossed about by the waves.

As the three boats pulled away from the ship's side a fourth pulled around from under the stern. Ahab stood beside the Parsee and the Chinese manned the oars.

"Starbuck, Stubb, Flask, spread out!" shouted Ahab. But they did not obey the order.

"Captain Ahab——" began Starbuck.

"Spread yourselves!" cried the captain. "Give way, all four boats! Flask, pull out more to leeward!"

"Ay, Ay, Sir," cheerfully replied little King-Post, as he swept around his great steering oar.

"Lay back!" he called to his crew. "There! There! There again! There she blows, right ahead, boys! Lay back! Never mind those Chinese boys, Archie."

"Oh, I don't mind them, Sir," said Archie. "I knew about them all the time. I heard them in the hold. I told Cabaco here about them. They are stowaways, Mr. Flask."

"Pull, pull, my hearties! Pull! Pull! Break your back-bones, my boys! What are you looking at? Those lads in yonder boat? Tut! They are only five more men to help us. Never mind where they came from. The more the merrier. Pull, then, pull! Stroke! Stroke! That's the stroke!"

"Hurrah for the gold cup of sperm oil, my heroes," continued Flask. "Three cheers, Men! Easy, now. Don't be in a hurry. Snap your oars, you rascals! That's it! That's it! Long and strong! Give way there, give way! Pull, will you! Pull! Pull! Pull! Why don't you pull? Pull and break something! Pull till your eyes pop out!"

"Here!" and he whipped out a sharp knife from his girdle, "every mother's son of you draw your knife! Pull with the blade between your teeth! That's it! That's it!"

All of this was said in a tone that was part fun and part anger. Every oarsman pulled for dear life, as well as for the fun of the thing. All the time Flask looked lazy and unhurried. He acted like a charm on the crew.

Starbuck obeyed a signal from Ahab and pulled across Stubb's bow. When the boats were near enough to each other Stubb hailed Starbuck.

"Mr. Starbuck, ahoy! A word with you, Sir, if you please!"

"Hello!" answered Starbuck. He did not turn an inch as he spoke. His face was set like a stone, and he urged his crew in whispers.

"What do you think of those Chinese boys, Sir?" called Stubb.

"Smuggled on board somehow before the ship sailed,"

answered the first mate. "A bad business, Mr. Stubb. There are hogsheads of sperm ahead, Mr. Stubb, and that's what we came for."

"Ay, I thought as much," said Stubb to himself after the boats had pulled apart. "As soon as I saw them I thought so. That's what Ahab went into the afterhold for. They were hidden down there. And Moby Dick's at the bottom of it. Well, it can't be helped. Give way, men, give way! It's not Moby Dick today! Give way!"

———•◆•———

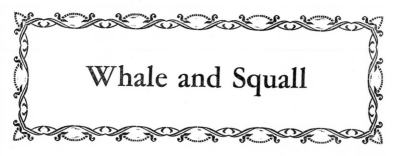

Whale and Squall

Ahab's boat pulled out ahead of the other boats. The members of his crew pulled as if they had muscles of steel. Their stroke was as regular as that of a trip hammer. The force of their stroke sent the boat shooting forward.

Fedallah, who was pulling the harpooner's oar, threw aside his black jacket. His chest and the upper part of his body were bare. At the stern of the boat Ahab handled the steering oar with the ease of a man with two good legs.

Suddenly Ahab's right arm was raised straight up. He held it there pointing to the sky. The boat's five oars came out of the water and were peaked. Crew and boat sat without moving on the sea. The other three boats stopped.

The whales settled down into the blue water. They gave no sign that they moved.

"Every man look along his oars!" cried Starbuck. "Queequeg, stand up!"

Queequeg sprang lightly to the raised box in the bow

of the boat. He stood erect while his eager eyes looked at the spot where the whales had last been seen. Starbuck balanced himself in the stern of the boat while it tossed and jerked. He remained silent while his eyes searched the vast blue of the sea.

As his boat lay still, Flask stood on top of a post some two feet high.

"I can't see," he said.

Upon hearing this Daggoo moved back and stood up.

"My shoulders," he said. "Will you mount?"

"That I will, and thank you."

Daggoo planted his feet firmly against two opposite planks of the boat. Daggoo held his hand for Flask's foot. With a spring and a toss his feet landed on Daggoo's shoulders. By holding one arm straight up Daggoo gave Flask a mast against which to steady himself.

At every roll of the sea Daggoo bent and rolled with it. On his broad shoulders Flask looked very small indeed.

Stubb, the second mate, did not care so much about the whales. He took his short pipe from his hatband, loaded it with tobacco, and struck a match. But, before he could take a puff, Tashtego, his harpooner, suddenly dropped to his seat and cried out, "Down! Down all, and give way! There they are!"

Just beneath the surface of the water the whales were swimming. They spouted water high in the air.

All four boats now headed for that spot of water. But it kept ahead of the boats since the whales moved on.

"Pull, pull, my good boys," said Starbuck in a low whisper. He did not say much to his men. He just looked straight ahead over the bow of the boat. Sometimes he would whisper an order or make a soft plea.

"Sing out and say something, my hearties!" bellowed King-Post. "Roar and pull! Beach me on the back of a whale. I shall go mad! See that white water!"

Shouting, he pulled his cap from his head, threw it down, and stamped on it. Then, picking it up, he threw it far out on the sea.

"Look at him now," said Stubb, the unlighted pipe between his teeth. "He's got fits. Soft and steady, my men. Pull! Keep pulling! Crack your backbones and bite your knives in two. Burst your livers and lungs—but, take it easy."

The sea rolled in great swells which made a hollow roar along the gunwales. Up, up one of the great swells each boat would go. It would pause a moment at the peak, then dip into the deep hollow between the swells.

With outstretched sails the *Pequod* bore down on the boats.

The boats pulled away from each other. A mist filled the air. The wind blew a gale. A squall was blowing up.

"Give way, men," whispered Starbuck, "there is time

yet to kill fish before the squall strikes. There's white water again!—close to! Spring! Stand up!"

Queequeg, harpoon in hand, sprang to his feet.

The oarsmen kept their eyes fastened on Starbuck's face. From the water came the sound of fifty elephants stirring in their litter. The boat boomed through the mist. The time had come.

"That's his hump. There, there, give it to him," whispered Starbuck.

There was a short rushing sound as Queequeg's harpoon darted from his hand. The boat shook with the shock of striking. It rolled and tumbled as though it had an earthquake under it. The boat was swamped. The crew was tossed into the whipping water. The whale escaped. He had only been grazed by the iron.

The men swam around the boat. They picked up the oars and tied them to the gunwales. They then climbed back to their places. The boat was half full of water. The men sat in it up to their knees.

The wind howled. The squall roared and cracked. Night fell over the scene.

There was nothing the men could do but sit out the night. They were wet, cold, and tossed by wind and waves.

As the dawn broke Queequeg started to his feet. He held a hollowed hand behind one ear and listened. A faint creaking came through the air. The sound came nearer. Suddenly the thick mist was parted by a huge form. The *Pequod* was headed straight for them. The men in the boat dived overboard into the sea.

For a moment the boat was beneath the ship's bows. Then the great hull rolled over it. It disappeared to come to the surface from under the stern later.

As soon as the boat appeared the men swam to it. The waves dashed them against its sides. But finally they climbed on board. Then the boat was taken up and landed on the deck of the *Pequod*. This was the last of the boats to reach the ship. The others had returned to the ship before the squall struck.

————•◆•————

Pirates and Whales

"Something in our wake!" called Tashtego from a masthead.

Captain Ahab swung around on his ivory leg. He pointed his glass at a half circle of white sails following the *Pequod*.

"Aloft there and rig whips and buckets to wet the sails!" cried Ahab. "Malays! They are after us."

The *Pequod* had rounded Cape Horn and headed north through the Pacific Ocean. By following this route toward Japan the *Pequod* would cover almost all the sperm whale waters.

Captain Ahab set his course through the straits which separated Sumatra and Java. This was a dangerous passage because the straits were the favorite hunting place of the Malay pirates. Also it was the favorite water of the sperm whales.

As the *Pequod* neared Java Head, a wonderful sight met the eyes of the crew. Ahead were the spouts of what seemed to be thousands of whales moving in a great half circle. Their spouts formed a long chain of sparkling jets in the sunshine. Each spout was a thick bush of white mist. They rose and fell, rose and fell away to leeward.

Full sail was piled on and the *Pequod* pressed after the whales. Moby Dick himself might be one of that great army of whales. It was as the ship crowded forward with all possible speed that Tashtego called out.

The pirates had lain hidden until the *Pequod* entered the straits. Now they came out in full pursuit of their prey.

As more sails were added, and all sails watered, the *Pequod* went faster. She flew through the straits to the safe waters beyond. The pirates were left behind.

The *Pequod* began to gain on the whales. They lessened their speed. Word was passed to make the boats ready. However, as soon as the boats were in the water the whales moved away with twice the speed at which they had been going.

For hours the sailors pulled after them. They were just about tired out when the whales again slowed down.

But something frightened the whales and they swam away in all directions. They were stricken with panic. Some thrashed about in their fright. Others floated helplessly on the surface. They were like sheep being attacked by a lion.

No matter how tired they were, the sailors rowed.

The boats separated and each was rowed toward a lone whale on the outer edge of the shoal.

Queequeg's harpoon reached a whale. At once, the whale, with the boat in tow, headed for the center of the herd. The boat and crew were in the greatest danger. They were dragged between the monsters who were thrashing and churning about. But Queequeg steered the boat clear of shining back after shining back. The boat was dragged to the very center of the great shoal of whales.

Starbuck stood in the bow, darts in hand. He used darts with the lines fastened to specially made blocks of wood. When a dart struck home, the whale dashed away. But he could not free himself from the block. It acted as a drag and held him back. Later the crew found the block and killed the whale.

One whale, with the dart in his side and the block of wood fastened to it, tangled the line with his tail. A sailor tried to cripple the whale by throwing a short handled cutting spade at its tail. The cutting spade worked loose and became tangled in the line. The whale went churning through the water, hitting hard with his tail. He was wounding and killing his own comrades. Mad with fear, all of the whales went tumbling toward the center, piling one on top of another.

Starbuck and Queequeg changed places.

"Oars! Oars!" whispered Starbuck grabbing the helm.

"Grip your oars and hold tight. Stand by, men! Shove him off! Queequeg, that whale! Hit him! Stand up! Stand up! Pull, men, pull! Never mind their backs—scrape them—scrape away!"

The boat finally reached the outer edge. The whales, all together, moved away. They swam fast.

———•◆•———

In the Cabin

"Who's there?" called Captain Ahab sharply without turning his head. A footstep at the door had disturbed him.

"On deck! Begone!" he bellowed without waiting for a reply.

The crew was pumping water out of the hold of the ship. They noticed that much oil was coming up with the water. The casks containing the whale oil must have sprung a leak. Everyone was anxious about having the oil loose in the hold. Starbuck went to the cabin to report this to the captain.

Captain Ahab was bent over his charts. He sat with his ivory leg braced against a leg of the table. In one hand he held a long jack-knife. His back was to the door. He wrinkled his brow as he traced courses on the charts.

"Captain Ahab mistakes. It is I," said Starbuck. "The oil in the hold is leaking, Sir. We must rig blocks and tackles and empty the hold."

"Rig blocks and tackles and empty the hold?" demanded Ahab as he started up from the table. "Do you want me to heave to here for a week to tinker a parcel of old hoops? And this, now that we are nearing Japan?"

"Either do that, Sir, or waste more oil in one day than we may make good in a year. That oil which we came twenty thousand miles to get is worth saving, Sir."

"So it is. So it is. That is, if we get it."

"I was speaking of the oil in the hold, Sir."

"And I was not thinking of that at all. Begone! Let it leak. What do I care? The hold is full of leaky casks. Those casks are in a leaky ship. Yet I don't stop to plug the leak. Who can find it in the deep hold? If it is found how can it be stopped? Starbuck, I'll not have the blocks and tackles rigged."

"What will the owners say, Sir?"

"Let the owners stand on Nantucket beach and yell. What do I care? Owners? Owners? You are always talking to me about those stingy owners. The owners are not my conscience. But look, you, the only real owner of anything is its commander. Listen, my conscience is this ship's keel. On deck!"

"Captain Ahab," said the mate whose face had turned red, as he moved further into the cabin, "a better man than I might overlook in you what he would not overlook in a younger man."

Ahab moved nearer to the guns.

"Devils! Do you so much as dare to judge me? Get on deck!"

"No, Sir, not yet. I beg you to be careful. Shall we not try to understand each other better than we have in the past, Captain Ahab?"

Ahab took a loaded musket from the rack in which the arms were kept. Pointing it toward Starbuck, he exclaimed:

"There is one God that is Lord of the earth, and one captain that is lord over the *Pequod*. On deck!"

The mate's eyes blazed and his face was red. As he left the cabin he stopped for a moment and said:

"You have not only insulted me, you have outraged me, Sir. But I do not warn you to beware of Starbuck. I warn you to beware of Ahab. Beware of yourself, old man."

"He becomes brave, but nevertheless he obeys. That is careful bravery," murmured Ahab as Starbuck disappeared. "What's that he said? Ahab. Beware of Ahab. There's something to that."

His forehead drawn into wrinkles, he walked to and fro in the little cabin. But soon the wrinkles in his forehead were gone. He returned the musket to the rack and went on deck. He walked to where Starbuck was standing.

"You are a good man, Starbuck," he said slowly. "I have decided to follow your advice."

Turning to the crew, and raising his voice he cried:

"Furl the topgallant sails! Close reef the topsails, fore and aft! Back the main yard! Rig blocks and tackles! Break out in the main hold!"

His orders were obeyed at once.

Queequeg's Coffin

The crew dug deeper and deeper into the hold. They brought out cask after cask of drinking water, bread, and beef. They hauled out bundles of staves and iron hoops. Everything was piled on deck until the sailors could hardly move.

Having so much cargo on deck made the ship top-heavy. The result was that she rolled badly. Luckily the sea was calm.

All hands worked below getting out the cargo. Harpooners as well as deck hands took their turns. Working in the cold and damp of the hold, Queequeg got a fever. Working in that damp, dark, unhealthy hold was like working in an icehouse. On deck it was hot. In the hold it was cold. Changing from one to the other gave Queequeg a chill. This was followed by a high fever. Even with the fever he stuck to his job. At last, however, it laid him low, and he took to his hammock. During the days that followed he wasted away.

After a while little was left of his huge body but the

frame and the tattooing. His cheek bones stuck out, and his eyes grew larger and larger. They had in them a softness which had not been there before. But as his eyes grew larger they showed a brave spirit that would not let him die.

Those who, from time to time, sat by his side were awed by the strange spirit they saw in his face. Death drew near as though to tap him on the shoulder and say, "Come."

He lay quietly in his swaying hammock. The rolling sea seemed to rock him to his final rest. The ocean's waves lifted him higher and higher toward heaven.

Every man in the crew gave him up. What Queequeg himself thought of his own case is shown by a request he made. In the gray morning watch, when dawn was just breaking, he called a sailor to him. Taking the sailor by the hand he said:

"When I was in Nantucket I saw some little canoes made of dark wood. It was the rich war-wood of my native island. I learned that when a whaleman died his body was laid in one of those dark canoes. I should like to be laid in one of those canoes. That is like the custom of my own people. When a warrior dies he is stretched out in his canoe and floats away to his heaven. I do not want to be buried in my hammock in the usual sea custom. I want a canoe like the canoes of Nantucket."

Queequeg's request was made known to the captain. He ordered the carpenter to make a canoe that would please Queequeg.

There was some old coffee colored lumber on board. It had been cut from the groves of one of the Pacific Islands. It was from these dark planks the coffin was to be made.

When the carpenter received the order he went to the forecastle and took Queequeg's measure. He chalked Queequeg's body as he moved his rule in making the measurements.

"Poor fellow, he'll have to die now," said the Long Island sailor.

The carpenter measured on his workbench the exact length the coffin was to be. He then got together the planks and his tools and set to work.

The last nail was driven. The lid was planed and fitted. He shouldered the coffin and went forward with it. As he went he asked if they were ready for it yet.

"Take that thing away," shouted the men on deck.

Queequeg heard the noise and asked that the thing be brought to him. There was no denying him. Everyone thought he was dying.

"Let him have his own way," they said.

Queequeg leaned over the side of his hammock. He looked keenly at the coffin. He then called for his har-

poon. He had the wooden stock drawn from it. He had
the iron part placed in the coffin with one of the paddles
from his boat. He then asked to have a flask of water
placed at the head. He wanted biscuits placed around
the inside edge.

A small bag of woody earth was scraped up in the hold.
It was put in a bag and placed inside the foot of the
coffin. A piece of sail cloth was rolled up for a pillow.

When all of these things had been done, Queequeg
asked to be lifted from his hammock. He wanted to be
placed in his coffin to see how comfortable it was.

For a few minutes he lay in the coffin without moving.

Then he asked a sailor to go to his bag and bring out his little god, Yojo.

He placed Yojo on his breast and crossed his arms. He asked to have the lid placed on the coffin. The head part of the lid had a leather hinge which fastened it to the lower part. The head part was turned back to let the crew look at his head and face.

"It will do," he murmured at last. "Put me back in my hammock."

Pip had been standing nearby. Before Queequeg could be moved Pip came forward and took him by the hand. In one hand Pip held his tambourine.

"Poor rover," he sobbed softly, "where you go now there will be no more travel. If the currents carry you to those islands where the beaches are only beat by water-lilies, do one little favor for me. See if you can find Pip for me. He has been missing a long time. I think he is in those far islands. If you find him, be good to him for he must be very sad. Look, he left his tambourine behind. I found it. Now, Queequeg, die, and I'll beat your dying march on the tambourine."

"I have heard," murmured Starbuck, gazing down the scuttle, "that men in high fevers have talked in ancient tongues. When the mystery is solved, it turns out that they had listened to those ancient tongues in early child-hood. I think that Pip speaks with a strange knowing of

Heaven. Where could he have learned of it except there? But he speaks more wildly now."

"We'll make a general of him," continued Pip. "Oh, I wish I had a game cock to sit on his head and crow. Queequeg dies game, mind that! But poor little Pip, he died a coward. If you find Pip tell everyone that he is a runaway and a coward. Tell them he jumped from a whale boat! I'd never beat my drum over Pip and call him General. No, shame upon all cowards. Let them go down like Pip who jumped from a whale boat. Shame! Shame!"

Queequeg lay with closed eyes, like one in a dream. Pip was led away and the sick man was put back in his hammock.

Now that Queequeg had made everything ready for his death, and his coffin had proved to be a good fit, he suddenly got better. Soon there was no need for the coffin. The men were happy that Queequeg was better. He said that when he was just about to die he remembered there was a little duty on shore for him to do. Therefore, he had changed his mind about dying.

"But can you decide for yourself when you are to live and when you are to die?" the men asked.

"Certainly," he answered. "If a man makes up his mind to live, a little sickness cannot kill him. Nothing but a whale or a gale can kill a man against his will."

In good time Queequeg regained his strength. One day as he sat on the windlass, he suddenly leaped to his feet. He stretched his arms and legs, yawned, and sprang to the head of his boat. Holding up a harpoon he said:

"I am fit for a fight!"

After this he used his coffin for a sea chest. He spent many spare hours carving figures on the lid.

Blacksmith and Forge

The weather was mild, and Perth, the blacksmith, had his forge on deck. The sailors and harpooners stood about, each awaiting his turn to have the blacksmith do some job for him.

There were weapons to be reshaped and furniture to be repaired. Holding their weapons the men watched every move of the blacksmith.

The old man used his hammer carefully. He was silent and slow as he worked over forge or anvil. The sweat poured off his face and his beard was matted. He wore a sharkskin apron.

At noon Perth was standing between his forge and anvil. He held a pikehead in the coals with one hand, while he worked the bellows with the other.

Captain Ahab, carrying in one hand a small leather bag, passed by. He paused as Perth drew his iron from the fire and began hammering it on the anvil. With each blow of the hammer sparks flew in every direction. Some of the sparks went close to Ahab.

"Are these your Mother Carey's chickens, Perth?" asked Ahab. "They always follow you. Look here, they burn—but not you. You live among them without ever getting burned."

"That's because I am already burned all over, Captain Ahab," answered Perth, resting one arm on his hammer. "I am burned so much already that I can't be burned any more."

"Your voice sounds too calm to me. You should go mad, Blacksmith. Say, why don't you go mad? What were you making there?"

"I was welding an old pike head, Sir. There were seams and dents in it."

"Can you make it all smooth again, Blacksmith, after the hard use it has had?"

"I think so, Sir."

"And I suppose you can smooth out almost any seams and dents, no matter how hard the metal?"

"Ay, Sir, I think I can. That is, all seams and dents but one."

"Look here, then," said Ahab, advancing and placing both hands on Perth's shoulders, "can you smooth out a seam like this?"

Ahab brushed one hand across his wrinkled brow.

"If you could do that," he continued, "I would gladly lay my head on your anvil, and take your heaviest hammer blows between my eyes. Answer! Can you smooth out this seam?"

"Oh, that is the one I said I could not smooth."

"Ay, Blacksmith, it is the one. It cannot be smoothed. What you see is the wrinkles in the skin on my forehead. But they have worked down into the bone of my skull. My skull is all wrinkles. But away with this child's play! You will repair no more gaffs and pikes today. I, too, want a harpoon made. I want one that a thousand fiends cannot break. I want one that will stick in a whale like his own fin bone. There's the stuff out of which to make it," and he flung the leather bag on the anvil.

"Look, Blacksmith, those are the nail-stubs of the steel shoes of race horses."

"Horseshoe stubs, Sir? Then you have here the best and toughest metal with which a blacksmith can work."

"I know it. Those stubs will weld together like glue. Quick! Forge me a harpoon! First, forge me twelve rods for its shank. Then wind, twist, and hammer those twelve together. Quick, I'll work the bellows!"

When the last of the twelve rods was finished Ahab tried them one by one. With his own hands he wound them around a long, heavy iron bolt.

"A flaw," he said handing back the last one. "Work that over again, Perth."

Perth, after working over the last rod, began welding

the twelve rods into one. But Ahab stopped him.

"I'll weld my own iron," he said.

Perth handed the long, glowing rods, one after another, to Ahab.

The Parsee passed silently. He bowed his head toward the fire in the forge. As Ahab glanced up the Parsee moved to one side.

"What's he dodging about for?" muttered Stubb who was looking on.

At last one of the rods was completed and received its final heat. As Perth, to temper it, plunged the rod hissing into a tub of water, the scalding steam shot up into Ahab's face.

"Do you want to brand me, Perth?" Ahab exclaimed as he winced with the pain. "Have I been forging my own branding iron?"

"I hope not" said Perth. "But I am afraid. Is this harpoon for the White Whale?"

"Yes, for the white fiend! And now for the barbs. You must make them yourself. Make them of my razors, here they are, the very best steel. Make the barbs as sharp as the edges of the razors."

Perth looked at the razors as though he would not use them.

"Take them, Perth. I shall not need them. From now on I neither shave, eat, nor pray until—go to work!"

Perth welded the arrow shaped tip to the shank. When he was ready for the last tempering he asked Ahab to place the water cask near.

"No, no! No water for that," exclaimed Ahab. "I want it to be of the true death temper. Ahoy, there! Tashtego! Queequeg! Daggoo! Will you give me as much of your blood as will cover this barb?"

He held it high. The three harpooners nodded their heads, "Yes."

Their skins were scratched until the blood came. The barbs intended for the White Whale were tempered in their blood.

Ahab now fitted a hickory pole to the socket of the iron. A coil of new rope was unwound and stretched with the windlass. Bending over it when it was drawn tight, Ahab twanged it like a harp string.

"Good! And now for the seizings," said Ahab.

When all was done Ahab walked away with the harpoon. The sound of his ivory leg, and the sound of the hickory pole dragging, rang along the planks.

The *Bachelor*

The *Pequod* went further and further into Japanese waters where the whales cruised. She met more and more whales. There were so many of them that the men spent from twelve to twenty hours at a stretch in the boats.

Sometimes they rowed, sometimes they paddled, and then again they just sat and waited for the whales to come to the surface. Although they did not have much success, they enjoyed being afloat all day. Their boats glided easily over the smooth, slow, heaving swells.

All seemed so secure and safe that it was difficult for the men to think of the ocean as ever being wild and dangerous. There were times when the masts of a distant ship seemed to be sailing through the tall grass of a rolling prairie, not through high swells of the sea.

It was a day, amid such scenes, that happy, jolly sights and sounds came bearing down on the *Pequod's* crew. The sights and sounds came from a Nantucket ship, the *Bachelor.*

She had just had the last cask of oil wedged in, and

had her bursting hatches bolted down. Now she was on
a glad holiday. She was sailing around among the widely
separated ships in the whaling waters before pointing her
prow for home.

Three men at her mastheads wore long streamers of
narrow red bunting fastened to their hats. A whaleboat,
bottom down, hung from her stern. The lower jaw of
the last whale the crew had slain hung from the bowsprit.
Signals, ensigns, and jacks of all colors flew from her
rigging.

Lashed in her three basketed mastheads were three
barrels of sperm oil. Nailed to her mainmast was a rare
lamp from a temple in Java.

The *Bachelor* had met with the most surprising success.
It was all the more wonderful because other ships, sailing the same seas, had gone for months without getting
a single whale.

The *Bachelor* had even given away barrels of beef and
bread to make room for the far more valuable sperm
oil. She had bought more empty casks from ships she
had met. These casks were stowed along the deck, and
in the captain's and officers' staterooms. Even the furniture of the cabin had been broken into kindling wood
to melt down the fat of the whales. The officers dined
off the broad head of an oil cask lashed down to the floor.
In the forecastle the sailors had filled their chests with

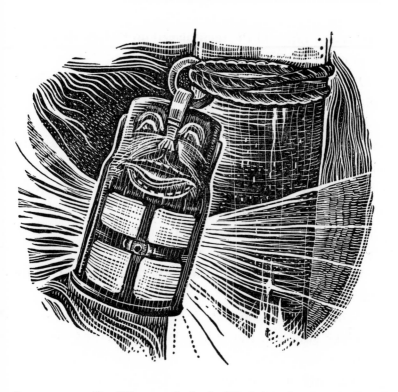

the sperm oil. The cook had filled his largest boiler. The steward had plugged the spout of his coffee pot and filled it. It was said that everything but the captain's pockets was full of sperm oil.

Such was the ship that bore down on the *Pequod*. The sound of big drums came from her forecastle. The drums were try-pots which had been covered with the skins of whales. The men stood around these and beat upon them with their hands. At every stroke the pots gave out a loud roar. Three of the men played on fiddles with shiny bows of whale ivory.

Other members of the crew tore down the bricks which held the fires over which the whale fat was rendered. The pots, which were being used as drums, had been removed. With wild cries the sailors hurled the bricks and mortar into the sea.

The captain of the *Bachelor* stood on the raised quarter-deck and watched.

Ahab, looking gloomy, stood on the quarter-deck of the *Pequod.*

As the two ships passed each other the *Bachelor's* captain called out:

"Come aboard, come aboard!"

"Have you seen the White Whale?" gritted Ahab in reply.

"No, only heard of him. Don't believe in him at all," said the *Bachelor's* captain in good humor. "Come aboard!"

"You are too good natured. Sail on. Have you lost any men?"

"Only two islanders, that's all. But come aboard, old hearty, come along. I'll soon take that black look from your brow. Come along! A full ship and homeward bound."

"So you're a full ship and homeward bound? Well,

then, call me an empty ship and outward bound. You go your way and I'll go mine. Forward there! Set all sail and keep her in the wind!"

While one ship went cheerily before the breeze, the other fought against it. As the ships parted, the crew of the *Pequod* looked serious, but the men of the *Bachelor* carried on their merrymaking.

Ahab, leaning over the rail, watched the homeward bound craft and took from his pocket a small vial of sand. The sand had come from the bottom of Nantucket harbor.

The Whale Watch

The crew sighted whales the day after the *Pequod* passed the *Bachelor*. Four whales were killed, one of them by Ahab.

When the bloody fight with the whales was over it was late afternoon. The boat pulled away from the whale that Ahab had killed. He sat and watched it as it died. As its life ebbed away it turned its head to the setting sun. Ahab said:

"He turns to the setting sun, slowly, but steadily. He honors the sun. He worships fire. His life goes toward the sun full of faith. But just as soon as he is dead, death turns the corpse and heads it in another direction. Then hail, forever hail, O sea, in whose eternal tossings the wild fowl finds his only rest. Though I was born of the earth, I have lived by the sea. The waves are my foster brothers."

After this outburst Ahab sat silent and watched the golden rays of the setting sun shine on the sea.

The four whales that had been killed died far apart.

They were scattered to the four points of the compass. One was far away to windward. The one on the lee side of the ship was closer in. One was out ahead, and one was astern.

Before nightfall the last three were brought alongside the ship. But the whale that was out to windward could not be reached until morning. Since Ahab had killed the whale, his boat had to stay by its side all night.

A pole was thrust upright into the dead whale's spout-hole. A lantern was fastened to the top of the pole. The light from the lantern cast a glare upon the glossy back of the whale. Its light also reached far out on the midnight waves.

The waves lapped gently against the whale's sides like soft surf upon a beach.

Ahab and the crew of his boat slept, all but the Parsee. He sat in the boat's bow and watched the sharks as they played around the whale.

Ahab was startled from his sleep by a moaning sound. The sound shuddered through the air. He sat up and found himself face to face with the Parsee.

"I have dreamed it again," said Ahab.

"You have dreamed of the hearses? Have I not said, old man, that at your funeral you may have neither hearse nor coffin?" asked the Parsee.

"May any one who dies at sea have a hearse?"

"What I said, old man, was that before you can die on this voyage you will see two hearses on the ocean. The first hearse is not made by human hands. The wood of the second hearse must be grown in America."

"A strange sight that will be, Parsee. A strange sight indeed will be a hearse with its plumes floating over the ocean, and with the waves for pallbearers. Ha! Such a sight we shall not soon see."

"Believe it or not, you cannot die until you have seen it, old man."

"And what was that saying about yourself?"

"That I shall go before you to be your pilot."

"And I understand that after you have gone before me to be my pilot, you must still appear to me before I can die. Was that not what you said? I have here two pledges that I shall kill Moby Dick and live."

"Then take another pledge, old man," said the Parsee whose eyes lighted up like fireflies in the night. "Only hemp can kill you."

"The gallows, you mean? I am immortal then, on land and sea," cried Ahab with a laugh. "Immortal on land and sea."

Both men became silent. The gray dawn came on, and the crew awoke. They arose from the bottom of the boat. The dead whale was brought to the side of the ship.

The Quadrant

Every day when Ahab came from his cabin he cast his eyes up at the sails. As soon as he appeared the helmsman would become very busy with the tiller.

The eager sailors would run to their braces and stand there with their eyes fixed on the gold piece nailed to the mast. They were anxious for the order to point the prow of the ship toward the equator. After a short time the order came.

It was almost noon. Ahab was seated in the bow of his whaleboat ready to take his regular daily study of the sun. He did this to find out just where he was on the ocean.

The ocean was like a sea of blazing glass. The sun was clear and bright. There were no clouds in the blue sky, nothing to soften the glare of the white hot sun.

Ahab's quadrant was fitted with colored glasses through which to look at the sun.

Ahab let his body roll with the roll of the ship. He held the quadrant to one eye. He waited for some moments for the exact instant when the sun would reach the meridian.

Ahab's attention was taken up with the quadrant. He did not see the Parsee kneel on the deck beneath him.

The Parsee's face was turned up like Ahab's, and he, too, eyed the sun. His eyes were closed to slits. His face was perfectly calm.

Ahab finished studying the sun. With a pencil he figured on his ivory leg his latitude at that very moment. He then looked up at the sun and murmured to himself:

"Oh, you high and mighty pilot, you can tell me where I am, but you cannot tell me where I shall be at any time in the future. Nor can you tell me where any other thing is at this moment. Where is Moby Dick? You cannot tell me, and yet you must be eyeing him at this moment. These eyes of mine look into your eye which is even now seeing him. And yet you cannot tell me."

Then, gazing at his quadrant, turning it over and over, he thought again, and muttered:

"You are just a foolish toy. You're a plaything for admirals and captains. The world brags of you, for your cunning and might. But, after all, you can do nothing except tell where you happen to be. You can tell nothing more. You cannot even tell where one drop of water or one grain of sand will be at noon tomorrow."

Ahab paused and held the quadrant up.

"Curse you, you vain toy," he continued. "Curse everything that draws a man's eyes up to heaven. Man's eyes were meant by nature to remain level with the horizon. If God had meant for man to look upon His heaven

He would have put eyes in the top of his head. Curse you, you quadrant!"

With this he threw the quadrant to the deck.

"No longer will I find my way by you! The ship's

compass and dead reckoning by log and by line shall show me my place on the sea."

He climbed from his boat to the deck of the ship. He stepped on the quadrant.

"Thus I stamp on you," he said, "and I split and destroy you!"

The angry old man stamped on the quadrant. As he did so a sneer of triumph passed over the face of the Parsee. Unnoticed, he rose and walked away.

The seamen crowded together on the forecastle. They scattered as Ahab shouted:

"To the braces! Up helm! Square in!"

At once the yards swung around. The ship wheeled on her stern. Starbuck watched the ship as she turned. He also watched Ahab as he moved along the deck.

"I have sat before a coal fire and watched it glow," said Starbuck to himself, "and I have seen it die down at last to ashes. Old man, what will remain of this fiery life of yours but one little heap of ashes?"

"Ay," cried Stubb, "but sea-coal ashes, Mr. Starbuck. Not your common coal. I heard Ahab mutter, 'Someone puts the cards into these old hands of mine, and swears I must play them and no others'."

Typhoon

As long as the weather was good and the sea calm the Japan Sea was beautiful. The skies were without clouds. Nothing disturbed their peace and quiet.

But back of this peace lay the most terrible of all storms, the typhoon. Sometimes it burst forth from a perfectly clear sky, like an exploding bomb upon a dazed and sleepy town.

Toward the end of the day the *Pequod* was struck by a typhoon. It came from straight ahead, and ripped the canvas from her masts, leaving them bare.

Darkness came on. Lightning flashed through the sky. Thunder roared.

Starbuck stood on the quarter-deck, holding tight to a rope. With every flash of lightning he looked up to see what further damage had been done to the rigging.

Stubb and Flask had the men lash the boats to make them safe. But their work went for nothing. They lifted the boats to the very tops of the cranes, but it did no good. Even Ahab's boat was struck by a great wave. It dashed up the side of the pitching boat and stove in the boat's bottom.

"Bad, bad, Mr. Starbuck," said Stubb looking over the wreck, "but the sea will have its way. I can't fight it. You see, Mr. Starbuck, a wave has a long start before it leaps. It runs all around the world before it leaps. But as for me, all the start I have to meet it is just across the deck here. It's all in fun, or so the old song says:

> Oh, jolly is the gale,
>
> And a joker is the whale,
>
> A' flourishin' his tail—

Such a funny, sporty, gamy, jesty, joky, hoky-poky lad, is the ocean, Oh!

> The scud all a flyin',
>
> That's his flip only foamin';
>
> When he stirs in the spicin'—

Such a funny, sporty, gamy, jesty, joky, hoky-poky lad, is the ocean, Oh!

> Thunder splits the ships,
>
> But he only smacks his lips,
>
> A tastin' of this flip,—

Such a funny, sporty, gamy, jesty, joky, hoky-poky lad, is this ocean, Oh!"

"Stop, Stubb," cried Starbuck. "Let the typhoon sing and strike his harp here in the rigging. But if you are a brave man you will keep quiet."

"But I am not a brave man. I never said I was a brave man. I am a coward, and I sing to keep up my spirits. I'll tell you what to do, Mr. Starbuck. If you want to stop my singing you'll have to cut my throat. When you do that, I'll bet you ten to one that I'll sing a hymn for the windup."

"You are crazy. Look through my eyes if you have none of your own."

"What? How can you see better on a dark night than anybody else?"

"Here!" cried Starbuck as he grabbed Stubb by the shoulder and pointed with his other hand to the weather bow.

"Do you not see that the gale comes from the eastward? It comes from the very course Ahab wants to follow for Moby Dick. That's the very course he headed the ship for at noon today. Now look at his boat there. Where is it stoved? In the stern, man, where he usually stands. Look! The place where he usually stands is stoved in! Now jump overboard and sing, if you must sing."

"I don't half understand you," said Stubb. "What do you mean?"

"Yes, yes," said Starbuck paying no attention to Stubb's question. "The shortest way to Nantucket is around the Cape of Good Hope. We can turn the gale that now hammers us into a fair wind that will drive us toward home. Yonder, to windward, all is blackness and doom. But to leeward, and that is homeward, it lightens up, and not with lightning either."

There was a flash of lightning followed by dense darkness. Thunder rolled overhead. At Starbuck's side someone spoke.

"Who's there?" he called.

"Old Thunder!" answered Ahab as he moved along to the pivot hole for his ivory leg. Suddenly a flash of lightning made his path clear.

At sea some ships carry a lightning rod fastened to each mast. This is to carry the lightning into the sea. The rods are made in long, slender links. They are kept on the deck until they are needed. Then they are thrown overboard into the water.

"The rods! The rods!" shouted Starbuck as a flash of lightning lit up the deck. "Throw them overboard, fore and aft! Quick!"

"Stop!" cried Ahab. "Let's have fair play here even if we are weaker than the elements. Let the rods be!"

"Look up!" called Starbuck. "St. Elmo's fire! St. Elmo's fire!"

Every yardarm was tipped with a pale fire.

Each three pointed lightning rod end was touched with three white flames. Each of the three tall masts was silently burning, like three candles before an altar.

"Blast the boat! Let it go!" cried Stubb as a wave heaved up under his own boat. He was trying to make the boat fast, and its gunwale jammed his hand. As he slipped back on deck he saw the flames.

"St. Elmo, have mercy on us," he pleaded.

Sailors swear a great deal and think nothing of it. They swear when the weather is peaceful and calm. They swear during a storm. They swear when they are hanging over the sea from a yardarm. But no sailor has ever been known to swear when God's burning finger has been laid on a ship.

While the fire was burning on the masts the crew said but little. They stood huddled together on the forecastle.

In the strange light of St. Elmo's fire Daggoo looked three times his real size. He looked like the black cloud from which the thunder had come. The parted lips of Tashtego let the light touch his white teeth. They shone as though they, too, had been touched by St. Elmo. Queequeg's tattoo marks stood out like blue flames on his body.

All at once the fire went out. The *Pequod* and those on her deck were wrapped in darkness. After a few moments Starbuck went forward. In doing so he brushed against some one. It was Stubb.

"What do you think now, man?" asked Starbuck. "I heard your cry, but it was not the same as it was in the song."

"No, it wasn't," answered Stubb. "I said, 'St. Elmo, have mercy on us.' I still hope he will. But will he have mercy only on long faces that do not know how to laugh? Hear me. Then take that flame at the masthead for a sign of good luck. Those masts are rooted in a hold that is going to be full of sperm oil. That oil will work up into the masts like sap working up into a tree. Our masts will yet be like three candles."

Stubb's face began to appear out of the darkness.

"See! See!" cried Starbuck pointing up.

Once more the flames were playing about the tops of the masts.

"St. Elmo, have mercy on us all," begged Stubb again.

At the mainmast, under the gold coin, the Parsee was kneeling in front of Ahab. However, his head was turned away. The seamen in the rigging hung like numbed wasps from a twig. Those on deck were fixed where they stood. All eyes were turned upward.

"Ay, ay, me!" called Ahab. "Look up at it. Mark it well. The white flame lights the way to the White Whale. Hand me those mainmast links there. I want to feel his pulse, and let my own beat against it. Blood against fire!"

With the last link held in his left hand, Ahab put his foot on the Parsee. His eyes were fixed on the flames, and his right arm pointed upward. He stood erect. He said:

"Oh, you clear spirit of clear fire. Once on these seas I worshiped you. You burned me so that, even to this day, I bear the scar. I know you, and I know that the right way to worship you is to defy you. You do not like love, and you kill those who hate you. It is no fearless fool who faces you now. I admit your great power, but I shall not let it master me. If you come in the form of love I will kneel before you. If you come in power and might I am not afraid of you. You made me of your own fire, and like a true child of fire I breathe it back to you."

Suddenly the nine flames leaped to three times their former height. Ahab, with the others, closed his eyes and covered them with a hand.

"You may blind me, but I can still find my way," continued Ahab. "You may burn me up, but I can then be ashes. The lightning flashes through my skull. My eyeballs ache and ache. My brain seems to be separated from my body and to be rolling on hard ground. Although I am blindfolded I will still talk to you. You are light leaping out of darkness. I am darkness leaping out of light. I leap with joy. I burn with you. I defy you, and yet I worship you."

"The boat! The boat!" cried Starbuck. "Look at your boat, old man!"

Ahab's harpoon, the one made by Perth, was lashed to its place in Ahab's boat. The point stuck out beyond the bow. The leather sheath had dropped off. From the keen steel barb there now came an even flame of pale, forked fire. The harpoon burned like a serpent's tongue. Ahab grabbed Starbuck by the arm.

"God is against you, old man," said Starbuck. "Stop now. This is an evil voyage, badly begun. Let me square the yards while we may. We can go on to a better voyage than this, and make a fair wind of it homeward."

The crew overheard what Starbuck had said. Although there was not a sail left aloft, they ran to the braces. They began to mutter among themselves. Ahab dashed the lightning links to the deck. He grabbed his burning harpoon. He waved it like a torch among the men. He swore he would stab with the torch the first sailor who touched a rope end.

The men were frightened at Ahab, but they were still more afraid of the fiery dart which he held. They moved back.

"Your oaths to hunt the White Whale are as binding on you as my oath is on me," said Ahab. "Heart, soul, and body, old Ahab is bound. That you may know the tune to which my heart beats I blow out the last fear. Look!"

With one breath he put out the flame. The men shrank from Ahab in fear.

Night Watch

Ahab stood beside the tiller. Starbuck came up to him and said:

"We must send down the main topsail yard, Sir. The band is working loose, and the lee lift does not work well. Shall I send it down, Sir?"

"Send down nothing!" growled Ahab. "Lash it! If I had skysail poles, I'd sway them up now!"

"Sir! In God's name!"

"Well, what now?"

"The anchors are working loose, Sir. Shall I get them inboard?"

"Lash everything! The wind rises, but it has not reached the height of my mind yet. Quick, do what I tell you! By masts and keels! He takes me for the skipper of some coasting smack. Send down my main topsail yard? My mind now sails among the cloud scud. Shall I send that down? Only cowards are afraid in a storm."

The anchors hung from the forecastle bulwarks. Stubb and Flask were lashing them down.

"You may pound that knot as much as you please, Stubb," said Flask, "but you will never pound into me what you were just saying. How long is it since you were saying just the opposite. Didn't you say that the ship on which Ahab sails should pay extra insurance? Didn't you say that if Ahab is on a ship it might just as well be loaded with powder barrels and matches? Now tell me, didn't you say so?"

"Well, suppose I did. What then? Can't I change my mind? Suppose we were loaded with powder and matches, how could they get on fire in this drenching spray? Why, my little man, you have pretty red hair, but even that couldn't catch fire now. Shake yourself. You're full of water. Don't you see that marine insurance companies have extra protection? Take your leg off the crown of the anchor so I can pass a rope around it. Now listen. What's the difference between holding a mast's lightning rod in a storm and standing beside a mast that does not have a lightning rod? Don't you see, you woodenhead, that no harm can come to the one who holds the rod unless the mast is struck first? What are you talking about then? Not one ship in a hundred carries lightning rods. Ahab was in no more danger than were the crews of ten thousand ships now sailing the seas. Why, you King-Post, I suppose you would have every man in the world go about with a small lightning rod running up from his hatband. Why don't you be sensible, Flask? Any man can be sensible."

"I don't know about that, Stubb. You will find it hard to do."

"Yes, when a fellow is soaked through it's hard to be sensible, that's a fact. I am soaked with this spray. But never mind. Catch the end of that rope and pass it back to me. It seems to me that we are lashing down these anchors as if they were never going to be used again.

Tying these two anchors, Flask, seems like tying a man's hands behind him. But the anchors are more like iron fists. And what a grip they have! I wonder if the world is anchored anywhere, and if it swings from a long cable. Hammer that knot down and we are through. I want to get back on deck. Wring out the skirts of my jacket, will you. I like a long tailed coat in a storm because the tails carry off the water. Hello, there goes my tarpaulin overboard! This is a nasty night, lad."

Tashtego was aloft on the main topsail yard passing new lashings around it. He muttered:

"Oh, oh, oh, stop that thunder! There is too much thunder up here. What's the use of thunder? We don't want thunder! Oh, oh, oh!"

The man at the tiller was thrown to the deck several times. As the wind and waves whipped the tiller back and forth, no man could hold it and stay on his feet. The ship was tossed about so much that the needles in the compass went round and round.

The storm did not let up until long after midnight. Finally Starbuck and Stubb cut what was left of the canvas away from the spars. Three new sails were bent and reefed. A storm sail was set aft.

Once more the ship went through the water as she had done before the gale struck her. When she was put on her course the helmsman could hold her there. During the worst of the gale he had not been able to steer at all. As he watched the compass he could tell that the wind was coming from astern. The breeze was becoming fair.

The yards were squared. The crew sang for joy.

"Ho! the fair wind!
Oh-he-yo, cheerily, men!"

Starbuck had orders from the captain to report at once, and every hour, any change on deck. Therefore, as soon as the yards were trimmed to the breeze he went below to report.

When he reached the door to the captain's cabin he stopped. Inside the lamp swung back and forth with the movement of the ship. Its light made shadows on the door. All was quiet.

In the light of the lamp a rack filled with guns could be seen on the forward bulkhead.

Starbuck was an honest and upright man. But the moment he saw the guns evil thoughts entered his mind. For the time being he did not know himself.

"Once he would have shot me," Starbuck murmured to himself. "There's the very gun he pointed at me. Let me touch it, lift it. Why do I shake so? I have handled many deadly lances, and I never before trembled. Is it loaded? Ay, it's loaded. That's not good. Shall I unload it? But wait, I'll cure myself of this. I'll hold the gun boldly while I think. I came to report to him a fair wind. Fair for death and doom, that's fair for Moby Dick. Ahab thinks it's a fair wind only if it leads to that evil fish."

Starbuck looked at the gun and at the door.

"That's the very gun he pointed at me, the one I have in my hand. He would have killed me with this gun. Ay, and he would just as readily have killed all his crew. He said he would not lower the spars in any gale. He broke his quadrant so that now he can only grope his way in these dangerous seas. In this very typhoon he swore that he would have no lightning rods. Shall this crazy old man be allowed to drag a whole ship's company down to doom? If this ship comes to harm it will be wilful murder of thirty men. The ship will come to harm if Ahab has his way. If he were done away with now he could do no harm to the men of the crew."

Starbuck took a long breath and looked at the gun in his hand. He then looked about him. He was excited and he was not thinking clearly.

"He is sleeping," Starbuck said to himself, "but he is still alive, and he will soon awake. I can't resist him when he is awake. He will not listen to my pleas. All he knows or cares about is to have everyone obey him. He says that we all took the same vow. God forbid! Is there no lawful way to stop him? Can we make him a prisoner and take him home? No, no one can take the power from his hands. Only a fool would try it. Even if he were chained down, he would be worse than a caged tiger. I could not stand the sight. I would not be able to get away from his howlings. I would not be able to sleep, and I should lose my reason. What can we do? The nearest land is hundreds of miles away, and it is Japan. I stand alone here at sea with two oceans and a continent between me and the law. Is heaven a murderer when lightning strikes a would-be murderer? Am I a murderer if . . ." and slowly, looking half sideways, he placed the muzzle of the loaded gun against the door.

"Ahab's hammock swings on a level with the muzzle of the gun," Starbuck continued. "His head points this way. A touch on the trigger and Ahab may not live to see his wife and child again. But if I do kill him, who knows but that all of us will go to the bottom today. Shall I? Shall I?"

Then he said aloud:

"The wind has gone down and shifted, Sir. The fore and main topsails are reefed and set. She follows her course."

It was as though Starbuck's voice had awakened Ahab from a dream. He started up shouting:

"Stern all! Oh, Moby Dick, I take you to my heart at last!"

The gun shook in Starbuck's arm. He fought with the angel of goodness and right. However, he turned from the door and placed the gun in the rack. The angel had won. Starbuck returned to the deck.

"Mr. Stubb," he said, "he's too sound asleep. You go down and wake him. I have matters to attend to here on deck. You know what to say."

The Needle

The following morning Ahab stood on the quarter-deck. Every time the ship dipped her bow he looked at the sun's rays ahead. When the stern settled in the trough of a great wave he turned to look back.

"Ha, ha, my ship," he exclaimed, "you might well be the sea-chariot of the sun. All you nations before me, I bring the sun to you. Hitch on the farthest waves, I drive the sea!"

Suddenly he stopped talking and hurried to the tiller.

"How is she heading?" he demanded.

"East-sou-east, Sir," answered the frightened helmsman.

"You lie!" shouted the angry Ahab, and he struck the helmsman with his clenched fist.

"How can you be heading east at this hour in the morning with the sun straight astern?"

No one had noticed that the ship was sailing in the opposite direction from that in which she should have been going.

Thrusting his head half way into the binnacle, Ahab took one look at the compass. One arm was uplifted. He let this arm fall to his side. He appeared to stagger.

Starbuck, who had been standing beside Ahab, looked and saw that the two compasses pointed east. Yet there was no question but that the *Pequod* was sailing westward.

Ahab gave a grim laugh.

"I know what has happened," he said. "It has happened before. Last night's thunder turned our compass around, that's all. I take it that you have heard of such a thing, Mr. Starbuck?"

"Ay. But it never before happened on a ship on which I sailed," answered the mate who was pale.

There have been ships struck by lightning which knocked down some of the spars and rigging. Where this happened the magnetic quality of the compass was entirely destroyed. Where this happened the needle could not be restored. If the binnacle compass is knocked out, so are all the compasses on the ship.

Ahab now stood in front of the compass. He looked at it. Then with the edge of his extended hand he took the exact bearing of the sun. He was satisfied that the needles were exactly turned around. He shouted orders for the ship's course to be changed. The *Pequod* swung around and once more her bow was pointed into the wind.

Ahab said nothing except to give the orders. Stubb and Flask went quietly about their duties. Some of the men grumbled. But their fear of Ahab was so great that they dared not stop working.

Ahab paced back and forth. His ivory leg slipped on the wet deck. He saw the crushed copper sight tubes of the quadrant he had broken the day before.

"You poor, proud heaven gazer and sun's pilot," he said. "Yesterday I wrecked you, and today the compass almost wrecked me! But I am lord over the level magnet yet. Mr. Starbuck, bring a lance without the pole. Also bring a top maul, and the smallest of the sailmaker's needles. Quick!"

Ahab was a very clever man. He wanted to impress the crew as much as he wanted to make a means of navigation. The old man knew that he could sail the ship with specially rigged needles. He also knew that the crew would look on what he did with superstition. This would add to his importance in their eyes.

Starbuck handed him the things for which he had asked. He then turned to the crew and said:

"Men, the thunder turned old Ahab's needles, but out of this bit of steel I can make a needle, and it will point as true as any."

The sailors looked at each other. Then they watched Ahab to see him work the wonder of the needle.

With a blow of the top maul Ahab knocked off the steel head of the lance. He handed the long iron rod to Starbuck and told him to hold it upright without letting it touch the deck. The mate held the rod. Ahab struck it on the upper end several times. He then placed the dull end of the needle on the top of the rod and hammered that. After he had done this he made some motions with the needle, and called for linen thread.

He moved the binnacle and slipped out the two needles that were no longer any good. Then over one of the compass cards he hung the sail needle.

The needle went round and round. At last, however, it settled in its place. Ahab, who had been watching closely, stepped back from the binnacle. He pointed to the needle and exclaimed:

"Look for yourselves and see if I am not the lord of the level magnet! The sun is east, and that compass proves it."

The men, who were ignorant of such matters, moved forward and, one after another, looked into the compass. As each man saw what Ahab had done he slunk away.

Ahab's fatal pride flashed from his eyes as he looked at the men with scorn.

Log and Line

"Forward there!" Ahab called to the Tahitian and the grizzly Manxman. "Heave the log!"

As he made his way forward, Ahab ordered:

"Take the reel, one of you! I'll heave!"

The log and line had not been in use. They had not been needed as the captain depended on the compass and his charts. The line was wound around a wooden reel. Tied to the line was an angular log. They hung just under the railing of the after bulwarks.

Since the log and line had not been in use it had not been touched. Rains and spray had kept them damp. The sun and wind had warped the log. All of the elements had caused log and line to rot.

Some hours after Ahab had repaired the compass he happened to glance at the reel. It reminded him of the broken quadrant, and of his oath about the log and line.

The ship was driving through the heavy seas, great waves rolling behind her.

After hearing Ahab's order the two men made their

way along the leeside of the deck. The sea, whipped to a cream, rushed by.

The Manxman took the reel. He held it high up by the handle ends of the spindle. The line was wound around the spindle.

Ahab went to the Manxman and unwound some thirty turns of the line. This would give him a hand coil to toss overboard. The Manxman watched Ahab and the line.

"Sir," he made bold to speak, "I don't trust that line. It looks far gone. Wet and the heat of the sun have spoiled it."

"It will hold, old man," answered Ahab. "Have wet and heat spoiled you? Maybe it is life that holds you, and not you who holds life."

"I hold the spool, Sir," answered the Manxman. "But let it be what my captain says. I am too old to argue, especially with my captain who wouldn't admit that he is wrong anyhow."

"What's that? Where were you born?" demanded Ahab.

"I was born in the little rocky Isle of Man, Sir."

"Excellent! The Isle of Man, eh?"

"Yes, Sir, I was born there."

"Well, here's a man from Man. A man born in once free Man. But what is it now? Up with the reel!"

Ahab heaved the log. The loose coils of the line straightened out astern. The reel began to whirl. The log was jerked, raised, and lowered by the rolling waves. This caused the Manxman to stagger.

"Hold hard!" bellowed Ahab.

Snap went the line. Away went the log.

"I break the quadrant," said Ahab, "the thunder turns the needles, and now the mad sea breaks the log-line. But I can mend anything! Haul in there, Tahitian! Reel up, Manxman! Look, you two, let the carpenter make another log, and you mend the line. See to it!" and he walked away.

"There he goes," said the Manxman, "and nothing has happened to him, but to me the bottom has dropped out of the world. Haul in, haul in, Tahitian! These lines go out whole and come in broken. Hey, Pip! Come!"

"Pip?" cried Pip himself, "you call Pip? He jumped from the whale boat. He's missing. Let's see if you haven't fished him up. The line drags so hard that he must be holding on to it. Jerk him, Tahiti! Jerk him off the line. We haul in no cowards here. Ho! his arm is just coming out of the water. A hatchet, a hatchet! Cut the arm off! We haul in no cowards here. Captain Ahab, Sir, here's Pip trying to get on board again."

"Peace, you crazy loon," cried the Manxman grabbing Pip by the arm. "Get away from the quarter-deck."

"One idiot scolds another," said Ahab as he moved forward. "Hands off him! Where did you say Pip is, boy?"

"Astern there, Sir, astern. Lo, lo!"

"And who are you, boy? Who are you?" asked Ahab in a kindly voice.

"Bell-boy, Sir, ship's crier. Pip, Pip, Pip. One hundred pounds of clay, five feet high, and easily known because he is a coward. Who's seen Pip, the coward?"

"Oh, Heaven, look down on this poor child that you have left alone," said Ahab. "Here, boy, my cabin shall be your home as long as I live. You touch my heart. You are tied to me by cords woven of my heart-strings. Come with me."

"What's this?" asked Pip as Ahab took him by the hand. "Velvet sharkskin. If I had ever known anything so kind perhaps I should not have been lost. This hand is to me like a life line, something a weak soul may hang on to. Oh, Sir, let old Perth come and rivet these two hands together. The black one and the white, for I shall not let go."

"No, boy, nor will I let go unless I see that I am about to drag you into something worse. Come, then, to my cabin. Come! I feel more proud of holding your black hand than I would holding the hand of an emperor."

"There go two crazy ones now," said the old Manxman

as Ahab and Pip went down the passageway to the cabin. "One is crazy with strength, the other with weakness. But here's the end of the rotten line, dripping wet. Mend it? I think we should have a new line. I'll see Mr. Stubb about it."

The Life Buoy

"Mermaids," said some of the men.

"Those were the voices of sailors newly drowned in the sea," said the old Manxman.

The *Pequod* followed her path to the equator. Ahab's needle and the log and line kept her on her course. It was a long way through little used waters. The trade winds and mild waves made it a tiresome one.

At last, however, the ship was drawing near the fishing waters of the equator. One night, in the deep darkness that goes before the dawn, the *Pequod* sailed by a group of rocky islands. Flask had charge of the watch on deck. Suddenly all were startled by a wild wail. So startled were they that each man stood, sat, or leaned against a support without moving. Thus they remained as long as the wild wail could be heard.

Ahab, in his cabin, slept through it all. The first he heard of the matter was when he came on deck.

"We heard the voices," said Flask. "They must have had some dark meaning for us."

111

Ahab laughed and said:

"Those rocky islands which we passed last night hold a large number of seals. Maybe some of the young seals had lost their mothers, or the mothers had lost their young. These mothers and the young seals came up near the ship and swam beside it. They cried and sobbed with their human sort of wail."

But many of the sailors had a feeling of fear about seals. This fear came not so much from the human cries of the seals as from the human looks on their faces as they looked up from the water alongside the ship. There had been times when seals had been mistaken for men.

The men felt that they were right to be afraid when, that morning, one of the sailors went overboard. The man who was lost had gone from his hammock to the forward masthead at sunrise. He was only half awake when he reached his station. Not long after that he cried out. Looking up, his fellow crew members saw his body sailing through the air. A moment later it disappeared in the sea. A heap of white bubbles marked the place where his body had struck the water.

The life buoy, which was lashed to the stern of the ship, was thrown into the water. But the life buoy had been allowed to hang in the sun. It was so dried out that the wood was shrunken and porous. As soon as it touched the water the dried wood filled and sank.

The sailor who was lost had been the first man to mount the mast to look for the White Whale, in the White Whale's own waters. The men looked on his loss as an evil sign put on them for hunting the White Whale. They said that now they knew the reason for the wild cries they had heard the night before.

"That is not so," said the old Manxman.

But the life buoy was gone. It had to be replaced. Ahab told Starbuck to see that it was done. But no cask for the purpose could be found. The men were ready to give up looking for one. By queer sounds and motions Queequeg made the men look at his coffin.

Starbuck stared in surprise.

"Use a coffin for a life buoy!" he exclaimed.

"Queer, I should say," remarked Stubb.

"It will make a good enough life buoy," said Flask. "The carpenter here can manage it."

"Bring up the coffin," ordered Starbuck. "There's nothing else to do. Make it, Carpenter, and don't look at me like that. Do you hear me? Make it!"

"And shall I nail down the lid, Sir?" asked the carpenter, moving his hand as though it held a hammer.

"Ay," answered Starbuck.

"And shall I caulk the seams, Sir?" and the carpenter moved his hand as though it held a caulking iron.

"Ay."

"And shall I cover the same with pitch, Sir?" and the carpenter moved his hand as though it held a pitch pot.

"Enough!" cried Starbuck. "Away with you! Make a life buoy of the coffin and say no more about it. Mr. Stubb, Mr. Flask, come forward with me."

"So he goes away in a huff," said the carpenter to himself. "Well, I don't like this. I made a leg for Captain Ahab, and he wears it like a gentleman. I made a coffin for Queequeg, and he won't put his head in it. Are all the pains I took with that coffin to go for nothing? Now I am ordered to make a life buoy out of it. I don't like it. I don't like it at all. It's not my place to do it. I only like to do jobs that begin at the beginning and end at the end. It's an old woman's trick to give me a mending job. Oh, well, I suppose I have to do it whether I want to or not. Now let me see. Nail down the lid. Caulk the seams and paint them over with pitch. Put canvas over them and fasten them down with strips of wood. Then hang the thing over the ship's stern."

He paused and looked at the far horizon. Then he resumed:

"Never before was any such thing done with a coffin. Who ever heard of a ship sailing about with a graveyard tray hanging from her stern? But never mind. I know what I'll do. I'll tie thirty life lines to the thing, one for each member of the crew. Then if the ship goes down there will be thirty sailors fighting for one coffin. Now I shall go to work on it."

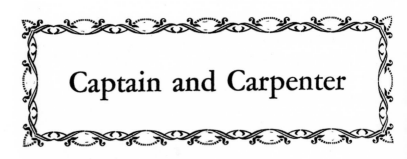

Captain and Carpenter

"Go back, lad, I will be with you again in a short time," said Ahab to Pip who was following him up the passage to the deck. Pip turned and went back without a word.

"He goes," said Ahab to himself. "He obeys me as quickly as my own hand does."

As Ahab turned to go on up the passage he saw the coffin on which the carpenter was working.

The coffin was laid on two tubs. The carpenter was busy caulking the seams as Starbuck had told him to do. He had a large roll of twisted oakum in the bosom of his shirt. He slowly unwound this as he worked.

"What's this?" Ahab asked as he reached the deck.

"This is a life buoy, Sir. Mr. Starbuck's orders. Oh, look out, Sir, the hatchway right behind you!"

"Thank you, man," answered Ahab. "Your coffin lies handy to the vault."

"Oh, the hatchway, Sir. So it does."

"Are you not the leg maker?" demanded Ahab. "Look at this stump of a leg. Did it not come from your shop?"

"I believe it did, Sir. Does it hold up, Sir?"

"It holds up well enough. But are you not also the undertaker?"

"Ay, Sir. I made this thing here as a coffin for Quee-queg. But Mr. Starbuck has set me to turning it into something else."

"Then you are an old scamp to be making legs one day, and coffins to bury them in the next. Then to be turning coffins into life buoys! You are a jack-of-all-trades."

"But I mean no harm, Sir. I just do what I have to do."

"Don't you ever sing while you are working on a coffin? They say that the Titans hummed tunes while they were carving out the craters of volcanoes. They say that the grave digger in Hamlet sings as he digs. Don't you ever sing?"

"Sing, Sir? Do I sing? Oh, I'm not much of a singer. The reason the grave digger sang must have been because there was no music in his spade. But the caulking mallet is full of music, Sir. Listen to it."

"Ay. That's because the lid on which you hammer is a sounding board. It's a sounding board because there's nothing under it. And yet, a coffin with a body in it sounds pretty much the same. Carpenter, have you ever helped to carry a coffin through a churchyard gate, and have it strike against the gate?"

"Faith, Sir, I've—"

"Faith? What's that?"

"Why, Sir, faith is only a sort of exclamation, that's all."

"U-m-m, well, go on."

"I was about to say, Sir, that—"

"Are you a silkworm? Do you spin your own shroud out of yourself? Look at your bosom! Hurry and get those traps out of sight!"

As he finished speaking Ahab went toward the after part of the ship.

"There he goes," said the carpenter to himself. "That was sudden. But squalls come sudden in these hot latitudes. The old man is always fiery hot. But he's looking this way. Come on, oakum, quick. Here we go again."

While the carpenter was talking to himself, Ahab was saying:

"That's something to see and hear. He is like a grey headed woodpecker tapping a hollow tree. I could wish that I were blind and deaf so I would not have to see and hear him. Tap, tap, tap. That is the way the seconds of a man's life are ticked away. A life buoy made of a coffin! Does it have some other meaning? Is the coffin in some sense a sign of eternal life? Will you never finish with that evil sound, Carpenter? I'll go below. I hope that he will be finished when I return. I'll talk this over with Pip. I get some wonderful ideas from him."

The *Rachel*

The next day a large ship, the *Rachel,* with many men on her spars, came straight for the *Pequod.* The *Pequod* was making good time through the water. But when the *Rachel,* with all her sails spread, shot between the wind and the *Pequod,* the sails on the latter ship went flat. It was as though the life had been knocked out of her.

"She brings bad news," said the old Manxman.

The captain of the *Rachel* stood with trumpet to mouth ready to hail the *Pequod.* Before he could say a word, however, Ahab's voice boomed out:

"Have you seen the White Whale?"

"Ay, yesterday," came the reply, followed by the question, "Have you seen a whale-boat adrift?"

"No," answered Ahab.

The captain of the *Rachel* stopped his ship. He went down the ladder lowered at her side. The sailors who manned his small boat gave a few swift pulls and brought the boat alongside the *Pequod.* As soon as the captain of the *Rachel* stepped on the deck of the *Pequod* Ahab knew

him. He was from Nantucket. But Ahab wasted no words in greeting. He went up to the captain of the *Rachel*.

"Where was the While Whale? He was not killed? Tell me about it," demanded Ahab.

"Late yesterday afternoon," said the *Rachel's* captain, "three of our boats were engaged with a shoal of whales. The whales led the boats four or five miles from the ship. They chased the whales to windward. Suddenly the hump and head of Moby Dick bobbed up out of the water to leeward. I had a fourth boat lowered and sent into the chase. This was my fastest boat. The man at the masthead said that he saw this boat fastened to the whale. He watched the boat go off in the distance. The last he saw was a gleam of white bubbly water."

The captain of the *Rachel* stopped speaking and looked out across the water. After a moment he went on.

"I had the recall signals placed in the rigging. I felt no fear for the boat. I picked up the other three boats. Then I started to look for the fourth boat. It had gone the opposite way. I crowded on all possible sail. I had a fire built in the try-pots for a beacon. I put every man aloft on the lookout. I have hunted all night for the missing boat. So far I have not seen her."

Again the *Rachel's* captain stopped speaking and looked at Ahab.

"And here is why I have come aboard your ship," he said as Ahab stood silent. "I should like for your ship to go with mine to hunt for the missing boat. The two of us can cover four or five miles as we sail along."

"I'll bet," said Stubb to Flask, "that some man in that missing boat took the captain's best coat. Maybe his watch was in it since he is so anxious to get it back. Who ever heard of two whale ships going after one missing whale-boat at the height of the whaling season."

But the captain of the *Rachel* was in earnest. He was so serious that his face was pale.

"My boy, my own son is among the crew of the missing boat. I beg you——" But again the captain stopped. Ahab said not a word.

"Let me charter your ship for forty-eight hours. I will pay well for it. You must, you must—you shall do this!"

"His son!" cried Stubb. "He's lost his son! I'll take back all I said. We must save that boy."

"He was drowned last night with the rest of them," said the old Manxman who was standing near. "I heard, you all heard their spirits."

Ahab stood like an anvil against the blows of a tiny hammer. The pleas of the captain of the *Rachel* did not move him. In one final plea to Ahab he said:

"I will not go until you say you will help me. Do to me as you would have me do to you if it were your son who is lost. You, too, have a boy, Captain Ahab. True, he is only a child, and safe at home. You will help! I see it. Run, men, run and stand to the yards!"

"Stop!" cried Ahab. "Don't touch a rope! Captain Gardner, I will not do it! I am losing time even now while I stand here talking to you. Good-by, good-by. God bless you, man, and may I forgive myself, but I must go on. Mr. Starbuck, look at the binnacle watch. In three minutes all strangers must be off the ship. Then let the ship sail as before."

He turned away his face and went down into his cabin.

The captain of the *Rachel* stood as though turned to stone. Then, stirring himself, he hurried to the ship's side and all but fell into his boat.

Each ship went its own way. The *Rachel,* and all her men, went searching the sea for the lost boat.

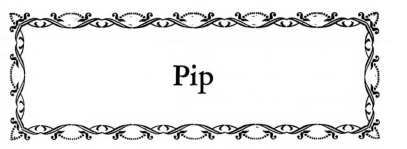

Pip

Ahab moved about the cabin getting ready to go on deck. Pip caught him by the hand.

"No, lad, you must not follow me now," said Ahab. "The time is coming when I do not want to scare you from me. Neither can I have you with me. You have something about you which helps to cure me of my sickness. But I need my sickness for this hunt for the White Whale. That's why I cannot have you with me. Sit here in my own chair as if you were captain."

"No, no, no! You do not have a whole body, Sir. Use me for your lost leg, let me be a part of you."

"If like cures like, Pip, then you grow sane again."

"They tell me, Sir, that Stubb once went off and left Pip. And yet Pip's bones are white even though his skin is black. But I will never go off and leave you, Sir, as Stubb did him. I must go with you."

"No, Pip, you cannot go with me."

"Oh, good master, master!"

"If you weep I shall slay you. Be careful because I, too,

125

am mad. Listen and you will hear my ivory foot on the deck. You will know that I am there. Now I go. Give me your hand. Shake. God forever bless you. God forever save you, no matter what comes."

Ahab left the cabin. Pip took a step forward.

"Just now he stood here," said Pip to himself. "But now I am alone. I do not even feel that I am here. Maybe this is only my spirit. It must be that the captain has cast a spell over me. He told me to stay here. He said this chair is mine. Here then I shall sit. I shall feel that I am an admiral. I shall have officers with gold lace on their coats at my table. It will be something for a boy to be host to officers. I shall say, 'Fill your cups, Captains, and let us drink shame to all cowards. I name no names, but shame upon them!' But I hear that ivory stump on the deck above. Master, master! I am indeed downhearted when you walk over me. But here I'll stay even though the ship goes down."

Ahab's Hat

The *Pequod* had now reached the very waters where Ahab had lost his leg. The *Rachel* had met and fought the whale that had taken the leg. It seemed only fitting that the whale should meet his end in these same waters.

Ahab's purpose was to kill Moby Dick. That purpose now shone from Ahab's eyes. The strength of that purpose kept the crew quiet. They dared not speak their doubts and fears aloud.

There was no more fun on the *Pequod*. Laughter had stopped. Stubb no longer tried to bring smiles to the faces of the men. Starbuck no longer needed to stop their smiles. All life on board seemed to be in Ahab's iron soul.

The men moved about the deck like machines. Ahab's eyes were always upon them.

But when Ahab was alone he was a different man. It was he who was afraid. He was afraid of the Parsee, just as the sailors were afraid of him. Fedallah, the Parsee, looked so strange that the sailors feared him. He shivered every little while. He did not sleep. For hours he would stand in one spot and shiver. His eyes held Ahab in their spell.

At any time, day or night, that the men came on deck, they found Ahab there before them. He would either be standing by the rail or pacing the deck. Sometimes he stood in the passageway to his cabin. At other times he paced back and forth. Always he had his hat pulled down over his eyes. The men could not tell whether or not he ever closed them. They could not tell whether he was sleeping or watching them. If spray or rain wet his clothing during the night the sun dried it on him the next day. Day after day, night after night, he stayed on deck. If he wanted anything from his cabin he sent for it.

He ate only two meals a day, and he had them on deck. His beard grew long, and it was matted on his face.

Ahab and the Parsee, although they spent all their time on deck, never spoke a word to each other. In some odd way something held the two men together. They would look at each other by the hour.

To the members of the crew Ahab seemed like a lord, and the Parsee his slave. It was as though the two were linked together by some power which drove them.

At the first sign of dawn each day, Ahab's iron voice would ring out: "Man the mastheads!"

All through the day, as the helmsman struck the bell for the hours, Ahab would call:

"What do you see? Answer, answer!"

Four days after meeting the *Rachel* no whale had been sighted. Ahab decided that he could not trust his crew. He trusted only the harpooners. He did not trust Stubb or Flask to report the whale if they saw it.

"I will have the first sight of the whale myself," he said. "I shall win that gold piece myself."

He decided to go aloft and look for the whale. With

his own hands he rigged a basket to haul him up. When all was ready for him to go aloft he stood and looked the crew over. His eyes swept from one man to another. He looked longest at Daggoo, Queequeg, and Tashtego. He did not once look at Fedallah. At last he looked at Starbuck.

"Take the rope, Sir," Ahab said to Starbuck. "**I give it into your hands.**"

Then Ahab sat himself in the basket. He gave the word for the men to pull on the rope and lift him to his perch. When he had been hauled up Starbuck tied the rope and stood near it.

With one hand holding the royal mast, Ahab looked for miles over the sea. He looked in a great circle made by his height above the sea.

It was the practice at sea, when a man was lifted to a point where there was no place for him to stand, the end of the rope which was fastened on deck was given in charge to some one man. This was done to keep anyone from making a mistake by setting the rope free. Such a mistake would result in the one aloft being cast into the sea.

Starbuck was the only one on board who did not agree with Ahab in everything. Therefore, it was strange that Ahab chose him to watch the rope. In other words, he entrusted his life to Starbuck.

Ahab had not been aloft more than ten minutes when a red-billed sea-hawk came flying and screaming around his head. It flew a thousand feet straight up, then it circled down around and around Ahab's head. But Ahab did not even see the sea-hawk. His gaze was fixed far away on the sea.

"Your hat! Your hat, Sir!" cried the seaman who was posted at the mizzen masthead. He was behind Ahab, and at a lower level. Thus he could see clearly all that was going on.

But the hawk swooped and, with his long hooked bill, snatched Ahab's hat and flew away.

The *Delight*

The days passed. The *Pequod* sailed on. The coffin life buoy swung lightly in place as the ship sailed over the rolling waves.

A ship, named the *Delight,* came near the *Pequod.*

"Have you seen the White Whale?" called Ahab as soon as the *Delight* was within hailing distance.

"Look," replied the hollow cheeked captain of the *Delight.* He pointed with his trumpet to the wrecked whaleboat on deck.

"Have you killed him?" demanded Ahab in an anxious voice.

"The harpoon that will kill him has not yet been made," answered the captain of the *Delight.* He looked at a canvas roll which some sailors were sewing together.

"Not yet been made!" cried Ahab in great excitement. He snatched up the iron which Perth had made. "Look at this, Nantucketer! Here in this hand I hold the White Whale's death! This steel was tempered in blood. The barbs were tempered by lightning. I swear to temper

132

them again in that hot place behind the fin where the White Whale most feels his evil life!"

"Then God keep you, old man. Do you see that?" and he pointed to the canvas roll. "Out of five stout men who were alive yesterday, all were dead before night. I can bury only this one. The others were buried before they died, buried by the whale. You sail over their grave."

The captain of the *Delight* then turned to his crew.

"Are you ready there?" he called. "Then place the plank on the rail. Lift the body."

He went toward the canvas roll with uplifted hands.

"Oh, God, may——" he began. But before he could say more a shout like lightning came from Ahab to his men:

"Brace forward! Up helm!"

But the *Pequod* could not move fast enough. Her crew heard the splash that the body made as it struck the water.

As the *Pequod* glided away the captain of the *Delight* saw the strange life buoy hanging at the *Pequod's* stern.

"Ha! Look yonder, men!" cried the captain of the *Delight*. "Those strangers can't get away from our sad burial. When they turn tail to us they show us their coffin."

Ahab Speaks

Ahab leaned over the side. Careful not to touch him, Starbuck went and stood beside him.

Ahab turned.

"Starbuck!" he exclaimed.

"Sir," replied the mate.

The day was clear. The sky was steel blue. The air was soft and pure.

Underneath the surface of the rolling sea, far, far down, rushed mighty sword fish and sharks.

Ahab crossed the deck and leaned over the side. From one of his eyes a tear rolled down his cheek and dropped into the sea. It was then that Starbuck joined him.

"Oh, Starbuck," Ahab said, "it is a mild, mild wind, and a mild looking sky. It was on just such a day that I struck my first whale. I was only eighteen, a boy harpooner at eighteen. That is forty years ago. Think of forty years of whaling, forty years of danger, forty years of the pitiless sea. For forty years I have left the peaceful land to make war on the evil creatures of the deep."

The old man paused and let his gaze wander far away over the water.

"Ah, Starbuck," he went on, "out of those forty years I have not spent three ashore. Ah, the loneliness of the life I have led. I have been whole oceans away from that young girl-wife I married when I was past fifty. I sailed for Cape Horn the day after we were married. She has been a widow with her husband alive. I widowed that poor girl when I married her, Starbuck. Since that time I have chased whales. What a fool, what an old fool I have been. Why this mad chase after a whale? I do not know for I am neither richer nor better for it."

Ahab paused, this time to look at the man beside him.

"Do I look old, Starbuck? Do I look so very, very old? I feel bowed and humped as though I were Adam. I feel old. Stand close to me, Starbuck, and let me look into a human eye. I see my wife and child in your eye. When I lower the boat to go after the whale, you stay on board. The danger shall not be yours. No, not with that far away home I see in your eye."

"Oh, my captain, my captain, noble soul! You grand old heart after all! Why should anyone give chase to that hated fish? Come, let us fly away from these deadly waters. Let us go home! Let me change the course and sail to Nantucket again. I think, Sir, that they have such mild blue days in Nantucket."

"They have, they have! I have seen them, some summer days in the morning. It's just about the time of day for my boy's mother to tell him of me. She will say I am abroad on the deep. She will tell him that I will come back to dance him on my knee again."

"My wife promised," said Starbuck, "that every morning my boy should be carried to the hill to catch the first sight of his father's sail. Come, my captain, study out the course and let us go home."

But Ahab's eyes were turned away. He shook as with a sickness.

"What is it that drives me on? I keep pushing and crowding and jamming myself on all the time. By heaven, man, it is fate that drives us. The air smells now as if it blew from a far-away meadow. Somewhere they have been making hay, Starbuck, and the mowers are sleeping in the new mown hay."

But the mate had stolen sadly away.

Ahab crossed the deck to look over the other side. He started back when he saw the reflection of two fixed eyes in the water there.

Fedallah, motionless, was leaning over the same rail.

———•◆•———

The Chase—First Day

That night, during the mid-watch, Ahab stepped out of the passage which led to his cabin. He went to the quarter-deck where he placed the end of his ivory leg in its auger hole. Suddenly he leaned forward and sniffed the sea air.

"A whale is near," he said.

The sperm whale gives off an odd odor which can be smelled at a great distance. Soon all the members of the crew could smell the sperm whale odor.

Ahab looked at the compass and made certain of the exact direction of the odor. He ordered the ship's course changed slightly, and the sail shortened.

At daybreak, right ahead of the *Pequod,* a long oily streak came into view.

"Man the mastheads! Call all hands!" cried Ahab greatly excited.

Daggoo hammered on the forecastle deck to waken the sleepers below. The men came running on deck, their clothes in their hands.

"What d'you see?" called Ahab turning his gaze to the forward masthead.

"Nothing, Sir," came the reply.

"Topgallant sails!" bellowed Ahab.

As soon as the sail was set Ahab cast loose the line which lifted his basket aloft. He ordered the sailors to pull him up. When he was only two thirds of the way up he gave a cry like a sea gull.

"There she blows! There she blows! A hump like a snow hill! It is Moby Dick!" shouted Ahab.

The three lookouts took up the cry. The sailors on

deck rushed to the rigging to see the whale for which they had been hunting so long. Ahab reached his perch which was five feet higher than the other lookouts. Tashtego stood just beneath him. From this height the whale could be seen clearly. He was about a mile ahead. His high white lump shone at every roll of the sea.

"Did none of you see him before?" Ahab called to the men around him on the yardarms.

"I saw him at almost the same instant that you did, Sir, and I cried out," said Tashtego.

"Not the same instant, not the same instant. No, the gold piece is mine. Fate kept the gold piece for me. None of you could have sighted the White Whale first. There she blows! There she blows! There she blows! There again!" Ahab cried, his voice keeping time with the whale's spoutings.

"He's going to sound!" shouted Ahab. "Down topgallant sails! Stand by the boats! Mr. Starbuck, remember that you are to stay on board and keep the ship. Helm there! Luff, luff a point. Steady, men, steady! There go flukes! No, no, only black water. All ready the boats there? Stand by, stand by! Lower me, Mr. Starbuck, lower, lower—quicker!"

Ahab, in his chair, slid to the deck.

"He's heading right away from us, Sir," cried Stubb. "He can't have seen the ship yet."

"Be silent, man," Ahab ordered. "Stand by the braces! Hard down the helm! Shiver her! Shiver her! Boats! Boats!"

The boats were dropped over the side. Soon the sails were set and oars working. The boats moved away, Ahab's boat leading.

As the boats came near the whale the ocean became smooth. It was as though some unseen hand had drawn a carpet over the waves. Ahab came so near the whale that he could see the whole hump. The whale's head was a little above the water. Ahab could see the wrinkles in his head. Bright bubbles rose and danced on each side of the whale. A lance which had recently been planted there stuck out of the whale's back. From time to time a sea gull would light on the lance.

Silently and calmly the whale moved on. The sea hid most of the whale's huge body and his evil jaw. But soon the front part of him rose slowly above the water. He waved his flukes in the air, dived, and went out of sight. The sea gulls hovered over the whirling pool that he left.

With their oars peaked and their sails flapping the sailors waited idly for Moby Dick to return to the surface.

"It will be an hour," said Ahab who was standing in the stern of his boat.

The breeze grew stronger. The sea began to swell.

"The birds! The birds!" shouted Tashtego.

The sea gulls, in a long single column, flew toward Ahab's boat. When they came within a few yards of it they stopped and fluttered over the water. They wheeled round and round making joyful cries.

Ahab looked down into the water and saw a white spot no larger than a man's hand. The spot rose toward the surface, growing larger and larger as it came nearer. Then Ahab saw plainly the long crooked rows of shiny white teeth. It was Moby Dick's open mouth and evil jaw. The great mouth opened wide under the boat. It was like the open door of a marble tomb.

Ahab gave a side sweep with his steering oar and whirled the boat aside to miss the whale. He changed places with Fedallah who was in the bow of the boat. He took Perth's harpoon. He ordered the crew to grasp their oars and be ready to back water.

By swinging the boat around Ahab had brought the bow face to face with the whale. Moby Dick shot his head lengthwise under the boat.

Moby Dick lay on his back and slowly took the boat between his great jaws. His lower jaw curved high up in the air, and one of the teeth caught in a rowlock. The inside of the whale's jaw was within six inches of Ahab's head. It reached higher than that.

The huge monster shook the boat as a cat shakes a mouse. Fedallah, his arms crossed on his chest, looked

calmly on this scene. The other members of the crew climbed over each other to reach the stern of the boat.

The whale played with the boat. He pressed the gunwales in and let them spring out. As he was under the boat he could not be harpooned by the men inside it. The other boats stopped to watch.

Ahab was maddened to have his enemy so close. He seized the long bone of the whale's jaw with his bare hands. He tried to tear its grip from the boat. But the jaw slipped from his hands and clamped shut. The gunwales bent in and snapped as the jaws came together. The boat was cut in two.

The members of the crew were thrown into the water between the two halves of the boat. The two parts of the boat floated apart. The crew clung to the gunwales of the stern and tried to hold the oars.

Ahab fell flat on his face in the sea.

Moby Dick moved away and lay with his head going up and down in the waves. He rolled over. His wrinkled forehead rose twenty feet out of the water.

Again he rolled over and swam around and around the wrecked crew. He churned the water as he swam. He lashed himself up to another and more deadly attack. The sight of the splintered boat seemed to madden him.

Ahab was half smothered in the foam made by the monster's lashing tail. He could not swim. He could just keep himself afloat. From the stern part of the wrecked boat Fedallah watched him. The clinging crew could do nothing to help him.

The whale swam in ever smaller circles. Would he swoop in on the crew?

The other boats were near, but they dared not move in close enough to strike. Had they tried to do so they would have been wrecked.

Starbuck, who had remained on the quarterdeck of the *Pequod* had seen all that took place. He headed the ship for the scene of action. As she drew near, Ahab, in the water, hailed her:

"Sail on the——"

But at that moment a sea broke over him and drowned his command.

He struggled from under the water. He managed to rise on the crest of a tall wave. He shouted:

"Sail on the whale! Drive him off!"

The *Pequod* sailed between Ahab and the whale. As the angry whale swam away the boats flew to the rescue of their captain.

He was dragged into Stubb's boat. The salt sea had blinded him. His eyes were bloodshot. The salt was caking in the wrinkles of his face. The men laid his helpless body on the bottom of the boat.

Ahab's body was weakened by the struggle through

which he had passed, but his heart was as stout as ever. He dragged himself up on one elbow and demanded:

"The harpoon, is it safe?"

"Ay, Sir, here it is," said Stubb holding it out.

"Lay it before me. Are any of the men missing?"

"One, two, three, four, five; there were five oars, Sir, and here are five men."

"That's good. Help me, man, I wish to stand. I see him. There he goes to leeward. What a leaping spout! Hands off me! I am myself again! Set the sail! Out oars! The helm!"

But with two crews in one boat Ahab could not hope to overtake the whale. The ship itself offered the only means for a successful chase. The boats returned to the ship. Even the boat that had been wrecked was taken on board.

With all sails holding the breeze the *Pequod* followed Moby Dick. Every time he spouted, the men who manned the mastheads called out. Each time the whale went below the surface Ahab noted the exact time. Then with binnacle watch in hand, he waited for the whale to return to the surface. When the hour of waiting was up Ahab shouted:

"Do you see him?"

If the answer was, "No, Sir," Ahab had himself lifted to his perch.

On deck he paced back and forth. He stopped before the wrecked boat. On his face was a deep frown. Stubb stopped near the captain. Trying to be funny he said:

"The donkey refused the Thistle because it stung his mouth, ha! ha!"

"Have you no soul to laugh before a wreck? If I did not know you to be brave and fearless, I could swear you are a fool. Neither groan nor laugh should be heard near a wreck."

"Ay, Sir," said Starbuck coming near, "it is a solemn sight, and it is an ill omen."

"Omen? That's only a dictionary word. I don't believe in omens. Begone! You two are just the opposite of each other. You represent all mankind. Among the millions of people on the earth I stand alone. Aloft there! Do you see him? Sing out every time he spouts, even if it's ten times a second!"

But the day was almost done. There was no longer light enough for the lookouts to see.

"How was he heading when you last saw him?" Ahab asked one of the lookouts.

"Straight to leeward, Sir."

"Good! He will travel more slowly now that it is night. Down royals and topgallant stunsails, Mr. Starbuck. We must not run over him before morning. He is making a passage now, and he may stop for a while. Helm there!

Keep her full before the wind. Aloft, come down! Mr. Stubb, send a fresh man to the fore masthead. See that it is manned until morning.

Ahab went toward the gold piece on the mainmast and said:

"Men, this gold is mine, for I earned it. However, I will let it stay here until the White Whale is dead. Whoever sees him first on the day he dies gets the gold piece. If I see him first on that day, then ten times the amount of the gold piece shall be divided among you. Away now! Mr. Starbuck, the deck is yours."

He stopped half way down the passage to his cabin. He stood there until dawn.

The Chase—Second Day

At daybreak three fresh men manned the mastheads.

"Do you see him?" demanded Ahab as the light of day spread over the water.

"See nothing, Sir," came the response.

"All hands on deck and make sail! He travels faster than I thought he would. The topgallant sails! Ay, they have been kept on her all night. But no matter, she has been resting for the rush."

"By salt and hemp!" cried Stubb. "This swift motion of the deck creeps up one's legs and tingles his heart. The ship and I are two brave fellows! Ha! Ha! We leave no dust behind!"

"There she blows!—she blows!—she blows!—right ahead!" was the cry from the masthead.

"Ay, ay!" cried Stubb. "I knew it, you can't get away! Blow and split your spout, O Whale! The mad Ahab is after you. Ahab will have your blood!"

The crew worked together as one man. They were like the ship, all welded together to make one whole.

All of the members of the crew were in the rigging. Some clung to a spar with one hand. Some waved a hand in the air. Some sat far out on the yards. All were ready for what fate might bring them. Each man was trying to sight the thing that might kill him.

"If you see him, why don't you sing out," called Ahab after waiting some minutes for further word of the whale.

"Swing me up, men," cried Ahab. "You are wrong. Moby Dick does not send up just one jet and leave."

Suddenly, less than a mile away, Moby Dick burst into view. The men gave a mighty shout. As the White Whale rose swiftly from the deep water, his whole body came above the surface piling up a mountain of foam.

"Your hour has come, Moby Dick," cried Ahab. "The harpoon which will end your life is here. Down! Down all of you, but one man at the foremast! The boats! Stand by!"

The men slid quickly to the deck. Ahab was lowered from his perch.

"Lower away!" he shouted as soon as he reached his boat. It was a spare one that had been made ready the day before.

"Mr. Starbuck, the ship is yours," Ahab called. "Keep away from the boats, but stay near them. Lower all!"

Moby Dick started for the boats. Ahab's boat was in the middle. He ordered, "Pull straight for his head."

The White Whale rushed among the boats with open jaws and lashing tail. Harpoons were darted at him from every boat. He paid no attention to them. He fought to destroy the boats. But they were manned by experts who kept the boats out of his way.

The whale darted this way and that. He thrashed about until the lines of the three boats were badly tangled. This shortened the lines and pulled the boats nearer and nearer to the whale. He moved a little to one side to make a greater charge on the boats. Ahab gave out more line. Then he pulled and jerked on it.

Ahab's line caught on the harpoons and lances which stuck from the whale's side. Suddenly these harpoons and lances came up beside the bow of Ahab's boat. With a boat knife he reached in among the steel rods and cut the line. The whale made a sudden rush among the other lines. This dragged the two boats commanded by Stubb and Flask near his flukes. He dashed the two boats together, splintering them. Then he dived. This left the two boats to be turned around and around in the whirlpool which he left behind.

The men from the boats grabbed at any part of the wreckage that came near them.

As yet Ahab's boat was not touched. He had the boat pulled toward the whirlpool to save anyone he could save. Suddenly his boat shot straight up in the air. The whale had dashed its broad forehead against its bottom. As the boat went up in the air it turned over and over. It fell back in the water, gunwales down. Ahab and his men struggled out from under it.

The whale moved a little away. He lay with his back to the wreckage. Each time any part of the wreckage touched him he drew back his tail and came on sideways.

At last, satisfied with what he had done, Moby Dick swam away, trailing the tangled lines after him. He moved away slowly.

Starbuck, who had watched the fight from the deck of the *Pequod,* sailed the ship to the rescue. He had a boat dropped over the side. While many of the men were hurt, no one was killed.

Ahab had clung to a broken half of his boat. When he was helped on deck, instead of standing by himself, he clung to one of Starbuck's shoulders. The whale had snapped off his ivory leg. All that was left of the leg was one short splinter.

"Starbuck," said Ahab, "there are times when it is good to lean on some one. I wish that I had learned to do that more often than I have done."

"The leg has not held up, Sir," said the carpenter coming near, "and yet I put good work into that leg."

"No broken bones, Sir, I hope," said Stubb.

"Ay! All splintered to pieces, Stubb. Did you see it?

But even with a broken bone I am not hurt. No bone in my body is more a part of me than the dead one I have lost. Aloft there! Which way?"

"To leeward, Sir."

"Up helm, then! Pile on all sail. Rig the spare boats! Mr. Starbuck, muster the boats' crews."

"First let me help you to the bulwarks, Sir," said Starbuck.

"Oh, that such a brave captain should have such a cowardly mate," said Ahab.

"Sir?" exclaimed Starbuck starting back.

"I do not mean you, man. I mean my own feeble body. Give me something that I can use for a cane. There, a lance will do. Muster the men. I have not seen the Parsee yet. Is it possible? Is he missing? Quick, call all the men!"

When the men were mustered, Starbuck reported the Parsee missing.

"Run, all of you, and find him!" cried Ahab. "Look everywhere! Find him! Find him!"

"He was caught among the tangles of your line, Sir," said Stubb. "I thought I saw him dragged under."

"*My* line! *My* line! Gone? Gone? There is death in that word, and I tremble. The harpoon, too. Turn over that litter and see if you can find it! That is the harpoon that was made for the White Whale. No, no! I threw it with my own hand. It's in the fish. Aloft there! Keep him in sight! Quick, all hands to the rigging of the boats. Get the oars! Harpooners, the irons, the irons! Helm there! Steady, steady for your life! I'll slay him yet, even if I have to sail ten times around the world to do it!"

"You'll never get him," said Starbuck. "No more of this. For two days you have chased him. Twice your boats have been splintered. Once more he has snatched your leg from under you. Your evil shadow, the Parsee, is gone. The good angels have warned you. What more do you want? Will you keep chasing this deadly fish until he slays the last man? Shall we be dragged to the bottom of the sea by him? Let's hunt him no more."

"Starbuck, of late I've been oddly drawn to you, ever since we looked into each other's eyes. But in this matter of the whale, your face is a perfect blank to me. The act must go on. I act under orders. See that you obey me. Stand around me, men. You see an old man who stands on one foot. What you see is only my body. My soul is like a centipede; it moves on a hundred legs. Before I break, you'll hear me crack. Until you hear that, you know that I follow my purpose. Moby Dick will rise to the surface once more—only to spout his last. Do you feel brave, men?"

"Ay, as fearless as fire," cried Stubb.

The men went forward.

"Ah, the things called omens," said Ahab to himself. "I try to drive out of other men's hearts that which sticks so fast in my own heart. The Parsee—the Parsee! Gone, gone. He was to go before me. But I was to see him again before I die. There's a riddle for you. I'll solve it, though!"

Toward evening the whale was still in sight to leeward.

The night passed much as the one before had done. The men worked most of the night repairing spare boats, and in sharpening harpoons for the next day.

The carpenter made Ahab another leg.

As he had done the night before, Ahab stood in the passageway to his cabin.

———•—•———

The Chase—Third Day

The morning was fresh and fair. Every man on board was on the lookout for Moby Dick.

"D'you see him?" called Ahab.

"Not yet in sight," came the reply.

"We're in his wake though. Follow that wake. Helm there! Keep on the course you've been following!" cried Ahab. "Aloft there! What do you see?"

"Nothing, Sir."

"Nothing! And here it is noon! The gold piece goes a-begging. See the sun. I've sailed over him. He's chasing me now, and that's bad. I might have known it, too. Fool that I have been! The lines and harpoons that he is towing! Ay, I've run past him during the night. About! About! All but the regular lookouts come down. Man the braces!"

The breeze had been driving the ship forward. She now turned about and headed into it.

"He now steers against the wind for the whale's open jaw," said Starbuck to himself. "God keep us. Already my bones feel cold within me. I am afraid that in obeying Ahab I did not obey my God."

"Stand by to swing me up!" cried Ahab. "We should meet him soon."

"Ay, Ay, Sir," answered Starbuck as he went to obey the order.

An hour passed. Suddenly Ahab saw the White Whale's spout. At the same time three shrieks went up from the mastheads. Ahab said:

"Forehead to forehead I meet you this third time, Moby Dick. On deck there! Crowd her into the wind's eye! He's too far away to lower the boats yet, Mr. Starbuck. Look at those sails, they shake! Stand over that helmsman with a top maul! Moby Dick travels fast. I must get down from here. One more good look around first, though. An old, old sight, and yet somehow so young; ay, and not changed a bit since I was a boy. What was that Fedallah said? He said that he would go before me, as my pilot. Yet he said I should see him again. But where? Good-by, masthead, keep a good eye upon the whale for me. We'll talk tonight when the White Whale lies down there, tied by head and tail."

He gave the order and was lowered to the deck.

The boats were dropped over the sides. Just before going into his own boat Ahab waved to Starbuck.

"Starbuck!" he shouted.

"Sir," replied the mate.

"For the third time my soul's ship starts on this trip, Starbuck," said Ahab.

"Ay, Sir, you will have it that way," replied the mate.

"I feel like a wave that has lost its force. I am old, Starbuck, shake hands with me."

"Oh, my captain, don't go," said Starbuck as their hands met.

Ahab tossed the mate's hand away from him.

"Lower away," he called. "Stand by the crew!"

A moment later the boat was pulled around under the stern.

"The sharks! The sharks!" cried the voice of Pip from the low cabin window. "Oh, my master, come back."

As soon as Ahab's boat was pushed from the ship, sharks rose from the deep waters beneath the hull. They began snapping at the oars. They followed only Ahab's boat.

"Heart of steel," said Starbuck as his eyes followed the boat.

The three lookouts at the masthead stood with arms pointing downward. That meant that the whale had gone under water.

But Ahab kept his boat moving. His men kept perfect silence. The waves hammered against the bow of the boat.

The waves swelled in broad circles. A rumbling noise came from down deep in the water. Suddenly a huge form shot up from the sea. There were many harpoons and ropes hanging to it. The form rose into the air, then fell back into the sea.

"Give way!" cried Ahab to the oarsmen.

The boats moved forward to the attack.

The White Whale was maddened by the darts that had entered his flesh the day before. Head on he came, thrashing his tail among the boats. He tore them apart spilling harpoons and lances into the sea. But Ahab's boat was left without a scar.

Daggoo and Queequeg were trying to stop the leaks between the planks. The whale showed one flank as he darted by them. The sailors gave a startled cry. Twisted and entangled in the ropes and harpoons in the whale's side was the body of the Parsee. His clothing was in shreds. His body was half torn in two. His bulging, dead eyes were turned full upon Ahab.

The harpoon dropped from the old man's hand.

"Ay, Parsee," said Ahab to himself, "I see you again. You have gone before, and that whale is the hearse you promised me. But I hold you to the letter of your word. Where is the second hearse. Away, mates, to the ship. These boats are useless now. Repair them if you can, and come back to me. If you can't repair the boats and come back, it is enough that I die. Down, men! I will harpoon the first man who tries to jump from this boat. You are

not as other men. You are my arms and legs. As such, obey me. Where's that whale? Has he gone down again?"

But Moby Dick was once more swimming steadily forward. He was swimming at great speed. He had his mind only on following his own straight course in the sea.

"Oh, Ahab," cried Starbuck, "it is not too late even now to stop. See, Moby Dick is not hunting you. It is you who madly hunt him."

But Ahab was far away from the ship and did not hear.

He had the sail set on his boat. It moved swiftly to lee-ward. As his boat passed the ship, Ahab could plainly see Starbuck's face. He shouted:

"Turn the ship about and follow me! Keep a safe space between us!"

Tashtego, Queequeg, and Daggoo were at the three mastheads. Ahab shouted:

"Tash, get a flag and nail it to the mast!"

The White Whale slowed down. As Ahab's boat sailed through the water the sharks were right beside it. They bit at the oars as they struck the water.

"Pull on," ordered Ahab, "never mind the sharks!"

"But the blades of the oars grow smaller and smaller with every bite by the sharks, Sir," said one of the sailors.

"The oars will last long enough," said Ahab. "Pull on! All alert now! We are coming near him. The helm! Take the helm! Let me pass!"

Two oarsmen helped him forward to the bow.

The boat came up beside the whale. But the whale paid no attention to the boat. The spray from his spout poured over the crew.

Ahab stood in the bow, both arms lifted high. At the right moment he threw his harpoon. With a curse, he sent it into the whale. As the iron sank to the socket in his body, Moby Dick rolled his side against the bow of the boat. Ahab barely missed being thrown into the sea by holding to the raised part of the gunwale. However, three of the oarsmen were thrown out of the boat. Two of them grabbed the gunwale and pulled themselves back into the boat. The third man kept his head above water by swimming. But the boat kept moving away from him.

The whale moved swiftly through the water.

"Take a new turn with the line," called Ahab. "Turn in your seats and tow the boat up to the mark!"

As the extra strain was put on the line it snapped.

"Oars! Oars! Burst in upon him!" called Ahab.

The whale whirled to face the attack. As he did so the ship came into his line of vision. Snapping his mighty jaws, he bore down on the ship's bow.

Ahab staggered and put the palm of one hand to his forehead.

"I am blind!" cried Ahab almost in despair. "Hold out your hands that I may find my way. Is the whale near?"

"The whale! The ship!" answered the seamen.

"Oars! Oars!" called Ahab. "Let me, this last time, reach my mark! I see! The ship! The ship! Dash on, my men! Will you not save my ship?"

The oarsmen forced the boat through the heavy waves. Already weakened by the blows of the whale, two of the bow planks gave way. The boat filled rapidly with water.

"The whale! The whale!" shouted Starbuck. "Up helm, you fools! The jaw! The jaw! Steady, steady! Up helm again! He is turning to meet us! May God stand by me now!"

"Stand by me, too," said Stubb, "for I stick here. I grin at you, you grinning whale!"

"Oh, Stubb," said Flask, "I hope my mother has drawn my pay before this. If she has not there will be little coming to her, because this trip is over."

The men gathered in the ship's bow. Each man held in his hand the tool with which he had been working when Starbuck shouted, "The whale! The whale!"

Moby Dick sent a broad band of foam before him as he rushed. With all the force he could command he hit the bow of the ship with his forehead.

The shock was so great that men reeled, and some even fell on their faces. Aloft the heads of the harpooners shook on their bull-like necks. The timbers of the bow were broken. Water poured in.

"The ship," cried Ahab from his boat, "that is the hearse, the second hearse! Its wood could only be American."

Diving beneath the ship, the whale ran along its keel. Turning under the water, he swiftly shot to the surface again. This time he was within a few yards of Ahab's boat. For a little time he lay quietly.

"Oh, my ship," said Ahab. "You with the firm deck, must you perish without me? Am I to be denied the last fond pride of the shipwrecked captain, that of going down with his ship? Towards you I roll, you undying whale. To the last I fight you. From hell's heart I stab at you. For hate's sake I spit my last breath at you. Since neither coffin nor hearse can be mine, let me be towed to pieces while chasing you, even though I am tied to you, you damned whale. Thus I give up the spear!"

Ahab threw the harpoon. The stricken whale flew forward. The line ran out of the groove with great speed, and it fouled. Ahab stooped to clear it, and he did clear it, but the flying turn caught him around the neck and drew him from the boat before the crew knew that he was gone.

For a moment the boat's crew was stunned.

"The ship!" shouted one of the men. "Great God, where is the ship?"

Only the tops of the masts were out of the water. The harpooners still stood at their lookouts.

As the ship went down she made a great whirlpool which sucked under the last remaining boat and all her crew. It took down each floating oar and lance pole, even the smallest chip from the *Pequod*.

Sea gulls flew screaming over the scene. The sea smoothed out and rolled on as though nothing had ever happened at all.

WORD LIST

accursed. Cursed, hateful.

aft. The back, or stern end of a ship.

after bulwark. The sides of a ship above the deck at the stern.

afterhold. That part of a ship below deck at the stern.

amazement. Great surprise.

anvil. An iron block on which metals are hammered.

astern. At or toward the back of a ship.

binnacle. A box, or stand, holding the ship's compass.

bowsprit. A pole sticking forward from the bow of a ship.

bulwarks. A ship's sides above the deck.

cargo. Freight carried by a ship.

casks. Barrels.

caulking. The cotton twist driven into the seams between the planks of a ship.

cloud scud. Clouds which move fast.

compass. An instrument for showing directions. The needle of a compass points to the magnetic north.

conscience. The feeling within which tells one what is right and what is wrong.

craters. The holes, or openings, at the tops of volcanoes.

crosstrees. Two pieces of timber placed side by side at a masthead.

elements. The forces of the air, especially in bad weather.

emperor. The ruler of an empire.

ensigns. Flags or banners.

equator. An imaginary circle around the middle of the earth, halfway between the North Pole and the South Pole.

eternal. Always and forever the same.

fate. A power that is believed to fix what is to happen.

feud. A long and deadly quarrel.

fin. The fanlike part on the back of a whale.

fluke. The rounded part of a whale's tail.

forecastle. The forward part of a ship in which sailors sleep.

forge. A furnace used by a blacksmith to heat metal very hot.

gaffs. Spears with barbs near the points to keep the fish from getting away.

hailing distance. The distance at which one person can hear another call.

halyards. Ropes used to raise and lower sails or flags.

harpoon. A spear with a rope tied to it.

harpooner. One who uses a harpoon.

hatches. The trap doors covering the openings in a ship's deck.

hemp. A rope.

hogsheads. Large casks or barrels.

hold. That part of a ship below decks in which cargo is carried.

horizon. The line where earth and sky appear to meet.

hornpipe. A lively dance.

huff. To puff up with anger.

idol. An image which is worshiped.

immortal. Living forever, a man's soul.

instinct. The will with which one is born to do certain things.

jacks. Small flags used for signals.

jibstay. For holding the jib sail.

lash. To tie.

latitude. Distance north or south of the equator, measured in degrees.

lee lift. The rope on the lee side which helps to raise or lower the main topsail yard.

lee side. Side of a ship sheltered from the wind.

leeward. Same direction as that in which the wind blows.

life buoy. A float for persons who have fallen into water.

litter. Young animals born of the same mother at the same time.

logbook. A book in which a record of everything that happens on a ship is kept.

lord. One who has power and authority.

magnetic. A magnet which attracts metals.

mast. A long pole of wood or steel set up on a ship to hold the sails, ropes, and spars.

masthead. The top of the mast.

meridian. A circle any place on the earth's surface passing through the North and South Poles.

mermaids. In fairy tales, maidens who are fish from the waist down.

Mother Carey's chickens. Sea gulls.

nail-stubs. The parts cut from horseshoe nails.

oakum. Hemp used for caulking the seams of ships.

pallbearers. Those who carry the body of a dead person in its casket.
Parsee. A person from India, usually from Bombay.
peak. The top of a great wave.
peaked. The tips of oars joining to form a peak.
perch. A seat high up.
pike head. The pointed steel head on a long metal or wooden shaft.
pikes. Long metal or wooden shafts with pointed steel heads.
pilot. A man who steers a ship.
plug. To stop a leak.
porous. Full of tiny holes.
premium. A prize offered.
prow. The bow of a ship or boat.

quadrant. An instrument for fixing the position of a ship.
quarter-deck. The part of the upper deck of a ship for the use of officers.

recognize. To see a person one has known before.
reef. The part of a sail that is taken in or let out.
reel. A round piece on which cord or rope is wound.
reflection. An image seen in a mirror or in water.
rivet. A bolt or metal piece with a head on one end.
royal yard. Yard arm which supports the royal topgallant sail.

scorn. To look down upon.
scuttle butt. A cask for holding water.
seizings. The cords used to tie things together.
shank. The middle part of a pike.
shark. A large fish that eats other fish and is said to attack people.
sharkskin. The skin of a shark.
shoal. A large number.
signals. Signs made to give notice of something.
smack. A small sailboat with one mast.

spars. Stout poles used to support the sails of a ship.
spell. A period of time.
sperm. Oil from the sperm whale.
spirits. Souls, ghosts, spooks.
squall. A sudden, violent gust of wind, often with rain.
stove boat. A boat that has had its sides smashed in.
strait. A narrow channel connecting two larger bodies of water.
superstition. Fear of what is unknown.
surf. The waves of the sea breaking on the shore.

tattoo. Coloring matter picked into the skin.
tempered. Steel is tempered by heating it and working it until it has the proper degree of hardness and toughness.
tiller. The handle used to turn the rudder in steering a boat.
Titans. Ancient gods.
top maul. A hammer.
trip hammer. A great power hammer.
try-pots. Vessels used for rendering the fat of the whale.
turban. A scarf wound around the head.
typhoon. A tropical storm in the China Sea.

vault. A grave.
vial. A small glass bottle.

wail. A cry of grief or pain.
wake. Track left behind a moving ship.
water butt. A cask for holding drinking or fresh water.
weapons. Something with which to fight.
weather bow. The side of the bow from which the wind is blowing.
weld. Join together by hammering while hot and soft.
windlass. A machine turned by a crank, for lifting or pulling.
windward. The side from which the wind blows.